# SOUL KISSED

Book One of The Moonstone Saga

By Courtney Cole

# Dedication

To my summer sister, Am.
Thank you for always believing in me.
And for putting up with me.
You're the best.

# Other Books by Courtney Cole

The Bloodstone Saga:
*Every Last Kiss*
*Fated*
*With My Last Breath*
*My Tattered Bonds*

*Princess*

*Guardian*

# Chapter One

I see colors. Blurs of colors blend together in distorted shapes, vivid and muted, light and dark. This is what always happens and so I immerse myself in the familiarity of it now as I allow my eyes to un-focus. As my reality becomes a colorful haze around me, I know it is for the best. I don't want to stare into this man's eyes as I kill him.

With a quick breath, I inhale his life. Even though it is feeble and sick and hollow, I allow it to slide down my throat, expanding my lungs with what was left of his vitality. In all honesty, there wasn't much there. Cancer had sucked at him for years, taking his strength and his will to survive. But this little puff of life was enough for me. It would sustain me for a few weeks.

I opened my eyes just in time to find his turning cloudy and I knew that he was gone. Fighting back regret, I straightened and gazed down at the man in the hospital bed, combing his blonde hair back with my fingers. He was slender and handsome, quiet and witty. I had truly liked him, as much as I dared to like anyone, anyway.

Divorced, 39-year old Daniel Delacorte. His daughter had died when she was only fifteen in a freak car accident. Apparently, she had been beautiful, vibrant and lovely. When she died, his will to live was buried with her. And then at that most inopportune time, right when he was drowning in grief, he had been diagnosed with stage IV cancer.

He wouldn't have lasted much longer, even without my interference. Mortal lives were so often tragic. I had seen the tell-tale weariness in his eyes a few weeks back when I had bumped into him in the hospital halls. It was the kind of weariness that only a person who was ready to die possessed, a haunting, bone-sucking exhaustion.

I had smiled at him and that was all. Then, because I reminded him of his daughter, he felt an instant connection with me. Little did he know that I would send him to meet her.

The door flew open and a team of nurses noisily shoved a crash cart in front of them.

"Move back," one of them ordered me as she yanked two paddles from an aging, yellowed machine.

Obligingly, I scooted against the wall. I felt nothing as I watched them work over Daniel's lifeless body, nothing as one of his hands dangled limply over the side of the bed. His fingers were pale. For months, he had been too sick to go outdoors into the sunshine. A normal person might have felt sadness at this, but I still felt nothing.

I had been doing this for so long. I had long since learned to harden myself against what I had to do. If I didn't, I would go insane. To survive, I embraced the numbness.

A doctor tiredly loped through the doorway, barely glancing at Daniel. The nurses had been futilely working for several minutes now. I knew it was hopeless and apparently, this exhausted doctor did too.

"Time of death?" he asked the closest nurse, the one wearing faded puppy dog scrubs. Her face was pained as she glanced up, first at the doctor and then at the clock.

"5:03."

They stopped working and the doctor turned to me.

"I'm so sorry for your loss, miss. There is a chapel down the hall and we can call a chaplain for you, if you'd like."

I shook my head.

"That's not necessary. I only met Daniel a few weeks ago, here in the hospital. He didn't have anybody, so I started visiting him here…" my voice trailed off.

The doctor briefly assessed me with trained, weary eyes. I honestly think he was too tired to care what my relationship was to his patient. He clearly needed a good night's sleep. After a moment, he nodded.

"Well, if you change your mind—" But he was interrupted as the door swung open and a boy stood in the doorframe.

My first inclination was to think *boy*, but he was probably eighteen or so. After being around for a thousand years, all mortal men began to seem like boys to me. Whatever his age, this one was handsome. Sandy blonde hair, warm hazel eyes, athletic tanned build. He was well-dressed in a pair of expensive jeans and a soft black leather jacket. His eyes were pretty and they widened when he saw Daniel.

The doctor turned to him.

"I'm sorry, you shouldn't be in here."

The boy straightened his broad shoulders and thrust out his chin. "He's my uncle. I'm Brennan Delacorte."

I was surprised, but tried not to show it. Daniel hadn't mentioned any other family. He always talked about feeling alone because of the loss of his daughter. He was divorced and no one ever came to visit him, so I honestly hadn't thought that he would leave a grieving family behind. I gulped and fought back guilt. I was definitely feeling something now and I didn't like it. This situation broke one of my own rules. I always aimed for men who would leave no one.

The doctor hurried to the boy. "I'm so sorry for your loss," he said quickly. "We did everything we could, but your uncle... well, I think he was just ready."

The boy nodded silently, his eyes frozen on his uncle.

"Are your parents with you?" the doctor asked. "You probably shouldn't be alone."

Brennan shook his head and swallowed, like he wanted to say something but couldn't trust his voice. And I couldn't help myself. The vulnerable, sad look on his face combined with my rush of guilt did me in and the words were out before I could take them back.

"I'll stay with him."

Brennan's head whipped around and I realized that he hadn't even noticed that I was in the room. His eyes widened again, but this time in confusion. I could practically see the wheels turning in his head as he wondered who I was.

"My name's Em," I explained softly. "I met your uncle here at the hospital a while ago. He was a really nice person."

"Yes, he was." Brennan relaxed. I could see it as his shoulders un-tightened. It never ceased to amaze me. My presence was soothing to mortals, it drew them in. In reality, it should alarm them, put them on edge and cause them to run far, far away from me. But they never did.

The doctor nodded and took his leave as the one lingering nurse straightened Daniel's blankets. With one last sympathetic gaze, she left Brennan and I alone.

I watched this boy curiously as he slowly approached his dead uncle. It had been so long since I had allowed my heart to warm to something. I didn't like it that way, but it was simply the way things had to be. It was interesting to me now to watch the sadness flit across this boy's handsome features. I felt a small twinge, somewhere deep within me, but I ignored it. I had gotten very good at tampering unwanted feelings down.

"I didn't know him very well," Brennan said softly as he picked up Daniel's limp arm and replaced it next to his still body. "After his daughter died, he kind of withdrew from the world. He thought no one understood. He stopped talking to my dad, and everyone else for that matter, and life went on without him."

"I don't think that he really wanted to go on," I offered limply. What else could I say? *I'm sorry, but I just shortened your uncle's already terminal life because I needed his soul?* Yeah, that would be an icebreaker, for sure.

"I know. He's been like that ever since Kayla's accident."

Brennan gazed down at his uncle and I paused at the expression on his face. He was still loving, still reverent, even though Daniel had shut them all out in his grief. It was fascinating. Mortals were so different from those in my world. But then, I had a father who was trying to kill me. That might slant my views somewhat.

"Are you, er, sick, too?" Brennan asked me hesitantly as his hazel eyes skimmed over my body. I knew he was searching for the tell-tale sickly, sallow look of a cancer patient. I shook my head.

"No. I volunteer here. I read to children, sit with sick adults, stuff like that."

Appreciation flickered on his face and I unconsciously took a step back. *No. Do not like me*, I silently commanded him. Not that it would work. Men were always drawn to me. They couldn't help it. It was one of my gifts. Or a curse, depending on how you looked at it.

"That's a very nice thing for you to do," he acknowledged softly. I saw the attraction in his eyes and I took a sharp breath. For some reason, his warm, vulnerable gaze appealed to me and I wanted to tell him that I was dangerous, to stay away. But of course I couldn't.

"It's not a big deal," I said instead. "I like it."

That wasn't the truth. I didn't like being here, because I only came here when it was getting close to time to feed. The hospital was the perfect place to find people on death's doorstep. It was the only thing I could do to assuage my guilt, to placate my conscience. If I took the life of someone who was going to die anyway, it wasn't really killing them, was it? That's what I told myself anyway.

I looked through the empty doorway, half expecting more of his family members to show up. "Is your father coming?"

Brennan shook his head. "No. And he doesn't know that I'm here. The hospital called this morning to tell us that Daniel's situation was serious. But my dad wouldn't come. They had some bad blood at the end."

"That's really sad," I murmured. "Your uncle was a good person."

"I thought you didn't know him very well?" he raised an eyebrow questioningly.

"I didn't. I'm just good at gauging people. It's a gift." I shrugged my shoulders. It was easy to gauge someone when you drank their soul and the very essence of who they were fed you. But I didn't mention that part.

"My dad's a good person, too," Brennan said. "But they're both stubborn. They both said harsh things and neither of them would take them back. And sometimes, when that happens with family, it's worse than with anyone else because you trusted them more to begin with. You know?"

He had no idea how well I knew. My own father had traded my soul for his own freedom from the Underworld, transferring his hateful curse onto me. I definitely understood familial betrayal. I lived with it every day.

I nodded. "I know."

Brennan gave me a sheepish look. "I'm sorry for telling you these things. I don't know what's wrong with me. I think just seeing my uncle like this... it was a shock..."

I almost took a step forward and put my hand on his shoulder and that inclination startled me. I knew better.

For anyone else, that would be a simple, harmless gesture. But not for me. I stayed where I was.

"I'm really sorry for your loss," I offered instead. "I know it's hard."

Brennan nodded wordlessly. He gazed at his uncle one more time before turning back to me. "Hey. Do you want to go down to the cafeteria and get a cup of coffee? I don't feel like going home just yet."

He was hesitant, but hopeful. Something about his voice reminded me of warm maple syrup. Warm and thick, yet somehow sexy at the same time. I felt the stirrings deep in my belly, the ones that urged me to step closer and inhale this man. I took another subconscious step back. Quickly.

"I can't," I answered. "I'm sorry."

Brennan studied me for a moment, his head cocked. I had definitely been wrong. He wasn't a boy. He had the serious gaze of a man. A stare like that could be dangerous.

"Please?" he added. "I'd like to be with someone who spent time with Daniel at the end. I can't explain it. I just want to make sure that he was okay. I won't take much of your time, I promise. Just one cup of coffee."

I had more time than he could ever imagine. I was immortal. That was a fact I reminded myself of as I stared at this appealing man-boy. Yes, he was handsome and sexy, but I could handle him. I could handle anything. My mother was the goddess of witchcraft, for Pete's sake- the most powerful witch in the world. Some of her strength had to have rubbed off on me.

I finally nodded. "Alright. Just one cup."

He smiled and I could swear the room brightened. I appraised his face quickly. Why was I drawn to him? I wasn't hungry. Physically, he was handsome. Classic features, healthy vibrant coloring. My pulse buzzed in my wrist, quick and feather-light. I swallowed hard. I didn't normally do this. There was no point. But for once, I listened to my heart, not my head. It would be nice to not be lonely for a few minutes.

Brennan held the door for me and I slipped past him, careful not to touch him. As I passed, though, I inhaled. He smelled delicious, like sunshine and man. A wave of weakness passed over me and I bolstered my self-restraint. *I would not hurt him.*

He punched at the elevator button and we waited, him patiently, me not-so-much. I had grown to hate the smell of hospitals, that sterile medicinal smell, and I wanted to leave here. Now. My purpose here was done and I wouldn't have to come back for a few weeks.

With a melodic 'ding', the metal doors opened and Brennan gestured me forward.

"Your chariot," he smiled.

I couldn't help but smile back. He had such an easy, laid back way about him. His spirit seemed almost gentle. And that seemed strange because he was so huge. I hadn't realized how enormous he was until we stepped into the elevator and I saw our reflections. The top of my head only reached his chest.

As we glided downward to the main floor, I discreetly looked at him in the mirror. He really was handsome. Broad, muscular shoulders, slim hips, sandy blonde hair that just started to flip upward at his neckline. It made him look a little mischievous. Warm hazel eyes that seemed almost like butterscotch and... were looking directly at me. He raised an eyebrow and I looked away quickly. He had totally just caught me giving him the once-over. Drat. That was the last thing I needed right now.

The doors slid open and he held out his arm.

"After you," he said quietly.

His voice was husky and I found myself wishing I could take a bath in it. It was gentle and sexy at the same time. As soon as I had the thought, though, I wanted to slap myself. What in the name of the gods was wrong with me? I had never been so affected by a mortal. Not ever.

As I stepped past him, he moved slightly and I bumped into him. Our forearms collided, the length of my arm from wrist to elbow pressed against him. White hot electricity jolted through me and I exhaled sharply, the breath seemingly forced from my lungs as my fingertips tingled. Brennan inhaled at the same time, his eyes un-focusing slightly from the contact.

*Shit.*

His aura appeared to me, a vivid array of colors and my breath hitched in my throat, my lips automatically opening just a bit. His energy was delicious, sweet and pure, and I was hard-pressed to pull away. As I slid my tongue along my bottom lip, I could taste it....I could taste him. His energy was incredible. I felt an almost uncontrollable need to draw nearer to him, just a little.

*I can handle it.* My own thoughts betrayed me.

Before I could help myself, I stepped closer like a moth to a flame. My lips hovered just a couple of inches from his and we lingered there, like we were the only two people in the world, drawn together by an invisible ribbon of energy. My heart took off like helicopter blades and I felt it thrumming in my chest, louder with each beat until it drowned out cognizant thought.

Brennan's hazel eyes stared into mine, the flecks of gold shining in the dim light of the elevator. I tried to focus, to concentrate on his eyes rather than the incredible pull that I felt toward him as I fought to gather the strength to move. I just needed to move away. It shouldn't be so hard.

But as I willed my feet to move, Brennan reached out his fingers and touched mine, fingertips to fingertips.

Sensations I'd never felt before, as soft as velvet but as strong as steel, flooded through my body, filling every vein, lifting me like I was floating on the swelling waves of the ocean. It was exquisite, unique and petrifying.

"What the hell?" Brennan murmured, his eyes still frozen to mine. His voice was quiet and raspy and filled with wonder, but it was enough to break my fixation on him and I yanked away, lunging out of the elevator.

"Wait!" he called to me, his urgency bleeding through his voice.

But I was already running down the hall. I had to get away from him. Far, far away before I hurt him. Curious nurses moved out of my way as I ran and I didn't look back even though Brennan was still calling my name.

I took the nearest exit, throwing the door open so hard that it slammed into the cinderblocks behind it and I flew down the stairs with the speed of the gods.

*What the hell was that?* I had never felt that way before in my life.

Typically, when I fed, I started the process at my will. It was a conscious effort, something that I could easily control. My self-restraint was never tested. It was just like kissing. I simply brushed my lips against theirs and sucked their souls right out of their bodies. It was quick and painless.

But with Brennan… I certainly had no intentions of stealing his soul, yet his aura had appeared with just my touch. He was young and vibrant and alive and I wanted him. I wanted him like I had never wanted anything else in my life. My need for him had filled me up, distracted me, overwhelmed me. I had never felt a connection like that before.

It was startling.

Amazing.

Terrifying.

Because it was incredible. Emotion had flooded my body, pulsing through my heart... waking it from an ever-long slumber. And because of that, I could never see him again. My curse made me dangerous.

I killed everyone that loved me.

# Chapter Two

The icy waves crashed against the shore of Lake Michigan, then receded back into the lake only to rear their liquid heads to crash again. The silvery light of the moon shone onto the surface, refracting against the rippling sheen like shattered black glass.

I sat on the top of a nearby bluff, inhaling the crisp night air and allowing it to rustle my hair from my shoulders, raising goose bumps along my bare arms. I always felt the best at night because the moon energized me. I literally felt stronger as the moonbeams caressed my skin.

There was a good reason for that. My mother, Hecate, was not only the goddess of witchcraft. She was also the goddess of the moon. Everything magical, dark or lunar-based fell within her realm. And by extension, my own.

"What are you doing out here?" a quiet voice asked from behind me. I sighed, knowing who it was before I even turned around. Ghosts fell within my mother's realm, also. And because of that, I could see them. Turning, I gazed at my friend Gaia, who just so happened to be one.

"I'm soaking in moonbeams," I answered. "What are *you* doing out here?"

Gaia's brown hair was coiled at her neck and she was wearing an elaborate ancient Roman dress because that is when she last lived. Not being able to change her clothes for the past couple of thousand years truly vexed her but she refused to cross over to the Underworld. She was terrified of the unknown. She was proving herself invaluable to me now though, as I tried to outrun my father.

"I'm just checking on you," she muttered as she perched on her heels next to me. "Why you like to sit out here in the sand, I'll never know."

"Why you hover above it like you're trying not to get dirty, *I'll* never know," I answered. "You're dead, you know."

"That hadn't escaped my attention," she smiled. And I had to laugh.

Gaia was slightly snobbish and pretentious, but that was just a product of her upbringing. Her father had been a wealthy Patrician and she had been born with a silver spoon clutched in her hand. She really did mean well. She had been with me for a while now, ever since she realized that I could see her. She stayed because she enjoyed living vicariously through me. She also enjoyed changing with the times. She had roamed the earth for two-thousand years as a spirit and her attitude and speech had adjusted accordingly.

"You really should cross over," I told her for the millionth time. "The Underworld isn't a bad place. I've been there. I should know."

"Really? If it isn't so bad, then why did you run from it?" she asked with her delicate eyebrow raised. The moon bathed her face in silver light. She wasn't beautiful, but she was a handsome girl with a lot of attitude. She was witty, funny and because of my present circumstances, she was my only friend.

"You know why," I muttered. "For one, I'm not dead. I'm a demi-god. There's a big difference. And two, my father, the evil soul-sucking, blood-drinker that he is, is trying to kill me so that he doesn't have to go back. He can find me too easily in the Underworld."

Gaia's features twisted into a delicate scowl, as she sat with skinny hunched shoulders.

"I still don't understand what exactly is going on. All these years and you've never really wanted to talk about it. Why did your father curse you?"

I stared at the water in front of me, watching as it peacefully ebbed and flowed, as I remembered my father's treachery. Swallowing hard, I waved my hand and my memories appeared in front of us like a shimmering movie. Gaia's eyes snapped as she leaned forward to watch.

I was with my mother that day and it was a beautiful, sunny afternoon. I was standing outside of her sparkling crystal cave while she had been bustling about inside. My father, Mormo, had appeared quietly, his long black duster swirling around him like mist. His face was pale, his hair dark.

"Hi, father," I greeted him uncertainly. It was unlike him to appear only to me. He had never shown much interest in me at all, he usually only visited my mother. I was an inconvenience to him.

"Hello, child," he replied solemnly, his pale face expressionless. "I need your help with something. Would you help your father?"

I could remember even now the cold pit that had formed in my belly. I knew that something wasn't right. But there was a magnetism there- he had drawn me to him and I couldn't resist. It was the same effect that I now had on others. It was part of the wretched curse.

Against my better judgment, I had taken one shaking step toward him. And that was all it took. Mormo whisked me away to the Underworld where we stood in front of the three Fates and Hades himself.

"You willingly offer your daughter to me, to stay with me here in the Underworld, in exchange for your freedom?" Hades had asked him, his face slightly incredulous. With his back to a flickering fire, Hades appeared even more handsome than he actually was, which was an impossible feat. He was heart-wrenchingly attractive.

Mormo nodded. "I bring her here to exchange for my own life."

The three Fates smiled in unison and I wanted to vomit. Even now, their treachery was unfathomable. They had willingly destroyed everyone.

"So be it," Hades replied grimly. "You may go. With my words, your curse has been placed upon your daughter Empusa."

Hades turned to me. "I'm sorry, Empusa. From this moment forward, you will carry your father's curse. You must consume the souls of mortals in order to stay immortal. You will drink the blood of mortals in order to remain young." He appraised me, his gaze almost kind. "I'm truly sorry, Empusa. Your father has a black soul. But I am sure that in time, you will find that you enjoy being here in the Underworld. I am not unpleasant and I am a good friend to have."

He had turned and left the room while I crumbled to the floor. To this day, I could feel the coldness that my father's betrayal had stamped into my heart. It had become a permanent fixture.

"And that's what happened?" Gaia whispered softly, startling me back to the present.

I turned to find her face frozen in an expression of horror. I could understand that. You couldn't fully comprehend the treachery of a father cursing his own child unless you had seen it for yourself.

"Yes," I replied numbly. "That is what happened. My father exchanged my life for his own."

"But your freedom was arranged…" Gaia trailed off.

"Yes, the goddess of peace did manage to arrange a deal to allow for my release, but I can't go in front of Hades again. I don't trust him."

"But your mother set up a meeting," Gaia argued. "All you have to do is show up."

It was my turn to raise an eyebrow. "Really? You think it is that easy? I should just trust Hades with my life—the god of the Underworld himself?"

She shrugged. "Your mother trusts the situation. I don't see what the alternative is. Running like this forever?"

It was a valid point, I'd give her that. I honestly didn't know what my end game plan was. I was too afraid to tell my mother where I was. I was afraid that she would immediately come to retrieve me and drag me into the Underworld to try and fix my situation. She had come to me in my dreams, but much to her agitation, I refused to give her my location. I trusted my mother with my life. But Hades… I did not trust him. I had seen enough of his actions in the Underworld to know that no one should ever trust him.

As I mused, I twisted the moonstone bracelet on my arm. My mother had given it to me the last time I had seen her. It was enchanted to alert me whenever my father was near. The moonstone was supposed to begin glowing. It was silent now, a pale, pearlish stone in the night. I never took it off. My life might someday depend on it.

"Something strange happened today," I murmured. Gaia's head snapped up.

"Oh? Such as?" She was always ready for a good story. Being dead bored her.

"I met someone."

I thought she was going to break her neck as she scrambled to my side, her elegant gown dragging behind her.

"Do tell," she purred as she scooted up next to me and tucked her legs beneath her. "What did he look like?"

"He was beautiful," I sighed, staring absently over the water. "Honey-colored hair, hazel eyes, perfect body. Tall, athletic."

She stared at me. "Could you be any more vague? How old is he?"

"I'm not sure. Maybe eighteen."

"Robbing the cradle, then?" she asked with a grin.

"Age is just a number," I replied glibly. "I look exactly his age. But it doesn't matter. I can't see him again. That's the strange part. I touched him on accident and I felt so drawn to him that I could barely move. I almost couldn't control myself. I wanted to inhale his soul."

"So what did you do?" Gaia asked with interest, her ghostly eyes gleaming in the moonlight.

"I ran."

"Just like that?"

"Just like that. What else could I have done?"

"Maybe you should have just taken his soul? Clearly, something was drawing you to him. Maybe you should have had a nice romantic moment and then sucked down his soul. Then you could have had a nice cigarette afterward and you wouldn't be quite so bitchy now."

"I don't smoke," I leveled a gaze at her. "And I'm not bitchy."

"Debatable," she declared. "But that's just a detail. Why do you always try so hard to fight your nature? You're supposed to drink souls. And I know that you drink blood in between. So, why do you fight it so much?"

"Because that's not who I really am," I snapped. "This is how my father has made me and I hate it. This is his curse to carry. I shouldn't have to carry it for him."

"And you wouldn't have to," Gaia answered calmly. "If you simply stood in front of Hades and asked him to reverse it."

"Easy for you to say," I grumbled. "You're already dead. You don't have to worry about someone killing you."

She laughed, a tinkling sound in the dark. "Regardless. You wouldn't have to drink blood *or* souls if you handed the curse back to Hades. Let your father deal with it."

"If only I could."

"This topic bores me," Gaia announced. "Let's get back to the mortal boy. You liked him?"

"Yes," I whispered and I watched her eyes glitter with interest.

Gaia knew it was against my rules to *like* someone, although she never could understand why I imposed rules on myself. In her opinion, gods were above the rules and shouldn't fret with them. But Brennan's face haunted me even now...that vulnerable, sad look. And he was so handsome that it made my stomach flutter.

"By the gods," Gaia murmured. "Our little Empusa is growing up."

I scowled at her. "I'm over a thousand years old. I'm quite grown."

"Didn't you say that age is just a number?" she asked innocently.

"You're awfully smart-mouthed for a ghost," I told her snappily. "Just so you know."

"Oh, I know," she confirmed. "What is the boy's name?"

"Brennan Delacorte."

"Delacorte? Wasn't that the name of the man who..."

I nodded. "Yes. I took Daniel's soul. He was Brennan's uncle."

"Oh, the tangled webs we weave," Gaia murmured. "It's probably best that you not see Brennan again. He might not be very understanding about the fact that you killed his uncle."

"Daniel was dying anyway!" I snapped.

Gaia knew I was sensitive about my situation, and she sometimes chose to rub it in just to annoy me. She had lost just a little of her mortal compassion since she had been dead for so long. Nothing bothered her anymore and she didn't hesitate to tick me off. She kind of liked it, actually. It spiced up her day.

She grinned. "Oh, I know. But that doesn't change the fact that you killed him prematurely!"

"Gaia, I swear to the gods—" but she was gone.

I looked around, but the only thing that surrounded me now were the empty sand dunes, silvery white in the moonlight. I sighed. She loved doing that- getting me worked up and then disappearing.

I trailed my hand through the sand, letting the fine grains fall between my fingers. Watching the tiny pieces fall into a pile onto the ground soothed my mind and I allowed myself to calm. I wasn't really sure why I was so worked up in the first place. Yes, it had been an odd incident. But I had been around for a very long time. In the scheme of things, it wasn't that big of a deal.

*Right?*

Then why was Brennan's face imprinted into my mind as if someone had burned it there?

Shaking my head, I crawled to my feet and stared once more out at the water. Because water was an element of the moon, I drew strength from it, as well. I knew that my mother would be searching for me next to the water but she would look in the coastal regions. That is why I chose to be near the Great Lakes instead. The lakes were large enough that they gave off a significant amount of energy, but I was counting on the fact that it wouldn't cross my mother's mind to search here…at least for quite a while.

I did miss her like crazy, though.

Turning, I trudged down the worn path back to the beach, then crossed the soft sand to climb the weathered wooden steps to my little cottage. The tiny gray Cape Cod home was nestled in a little patch of trees on a bluff overlooking the lake. I had been incredibly lucky to happen upon its owner in a tiny shop in town and had overheard him saying that he was going to be in Europe for a year and wanted to rent it out, fully furnished. I had jumped on that the second that I heard it. Like all men, he was immediately drawn to me and within five minutes, we had a handshake.

Flipping on the light, I entered the living room and dropped into the chair by the glistening bay window. Every window on the back of the house faced the lake and moonlight poured into each one. But this one was my favorite. I could curl up in the comfortable chair and bask in the moonlight all night long, if I chose. And from this vantage point I could see the stairs leading up to my house. If anyone walked up them, I would know.

I settled into the fluffy leather cushions of the chair and leaned my cheek against my knees as I drew them up to my chest. I had taken a soul tonight, so my weariness was gone. Daniel's soul would keep me thriving for a few weeks. But that wouldn't stop my actual hunger. To do that, I would need blood. Holding out a hand, I examined it. My skin was getting paler, a clear indication that I needed to eat. My stomach had been empty for a while and it burned right now from the emptiness.

Damn it all to hell. Once again, I cursed my father. This was so unfair. I had never, in my entire life, done anything to deserve this. Putting my agitation aside, I ran through a stack of various scenarios. Where could I eat? It didn't take long to figure out. It was 11:00 pm on a chilly October Friday. There would be teenagers building bonfires on the beaches. With a sigh, I uncurled myself from my chair.

Throwing open my closet, I pulled out a soft sweatshirt and warm cozy boots. If I had to go back outside, I was at least going to be warm. But for this mission, I needed to look sexy, too. Sighing again, I replaced the soft old sweatshirt with an off-the-shoulder gray sweater and skinny jeans. The boots, though… they could stay.

Pulling my hair out of the high ponytail that it was currently in, I ran a brush through the long dark length. When I was finished, it hung in a glossy sheen that just touched the middle of my shoulder blades. I didn't even look in the mirror. I knew what I would look like. My sweater would emphasize the fact that my eyes were gray, my shoulders were slender and my breasts were full. My skinny jeans would showcase my slender legs and hips. My complexion would be perfect, my lips soft and full.

Most women enjoyed being beautiful, but to me... well, I didn't enjoy it as much. It was just one more tool in my arsenal. My beauty drew men to me for a purpose that I didn't enjoy.

I slipped out the door and back down to the darkened beaches, quietly hunting for a bonfire like a hungry lioness. As my boots sunk in the soft sand, it didn't take long to see the tell-tale orange glow of the first fire. The kids around here so loved beach parties. I was fortunate, I appeared to be around seventeen or eighteen- the perfect age to attend either high school or college parties, whichever the need might be.

As I sidled up to the sprawling get-together, I was conscious of the fact that I was arriving alone. The teenagers around me were clumped into noisy groups of two or more. But there had to be a loner here somewhere. There always was. I scanned the perimeter and focused in on a skinny boy standing alone, holding a cup of beer. *Bingo.*

I made a bee-line for him, sliding up to stand very close to his elbow. He looked at me in surprise and was immediately flustered, not quite able to make eye contact. It was apparent that he was an outsider. He wanted to be here at the party, but he didn't have anyone to talk to. Until now.

"Hi," I murmured softly, moving closer to him. He wasn't ugly, but he wasn't handsome, either. He had light brown hair, blue eyes and pale skin. *Math geek*, I thought. He clearly didn't go out in the sun much.

"Hi," he stammered, his cheeks flushing crimson. He was definitely awkward around females.

"I'm new here," I continued, getting as close as I could to him without touching him. The wind picked up and I could smell my own perfume on the breeze, soft and feminine. He inhaled it, closing his eyes for a second. My nearness was already affecting him.

"You smell nice," he replied, re-opening his eyes. "Where did you move from?"

"From quite a ways away," I laughed. "So I don't know anyone. What's your name?"

"Jason," he answered shyly, his cheeks still pink. His blue eyes were glued to mine now. He was hanging on every word. This would be so easy. I sighed. I grew tired of this process. Boy after boy after boy.

"Well, Jason. I love the water. Would you like to take a walk with me?"

His surprised gaze flickered over mine. "Really?" he asked, then quickly followed up with, "Yes. I'd love to."

*Nice save*, I commended him silently.

I felt badly for him, actually. It was clear that he was painfully shy. This would be like taking candy from a baby. I laid my hand on his arm and the moment that I did, he was consumed with wanting me. I knew because that is what always happened. I knew because his eyes glazed over and became slightly unfocused.

I led him through the throngs of people and found that I slightly enjoyed the stares. At the very least, these kids would be talking about Jason tomorrow. They would wonder who the hot girl was that he had been with. I could at least do that for him. It was a small thing, but it was something.

I walked just far enough away from the water that I didn't get wet and I stared at the moon as we walked. I just needed a little bit of isolation. Just a little bit further.

"Why me?" Jason asked curiously, bringing me out of my thoughts. "Why did you choose me?"

I smiled. "Because you seem sweet."

He blushed again and fell silent, but stayed very close to my side. I looked behind us. There was no one in sight now so I wasted no time. I pulled him behind the nearest clump of brush. It was bristly and dry, but it would hide us from any straggling party-goers.

"Let's sit, okay?" I suggested as I tugged him to the ground.

But rather than sit, I pushed him softly onto his back into the sand and straddled him. His eyes widened and he fell slack as he waited for my next move. His hopeful breath froze in his throat. I reached out a hand and stroked his cheek, bending to whisper into his ear.

"You really are sweet, aren't you, Jason?"

He nodded, unable to speak. My close proximity was working its magic. I kissed his cheek and he closed his eyes.

"I need to tell you something, Jason, alright?" He nodded slowly with his eyes closed. His hands were laying limply at his sides- his inexperience showing itself. He wasn't even trying to touch me.

"You will probably fall asleep here in a little bit. When you wake, return to the party. You won't remember anything that happened here."

His eyes opened, un-focused and slightly confused.

"I won't?"

"No, you won't."

He looked disappointed, but the confusion soon clouded his face once more.

"Don't worry," I whispered as I kissed his neck. "I'll make it worth it."

He smiled slightly, still lost in his haze.

Bending, I grazed his lips with my own and then inhaled, just a little. One small mouthful was all it would take to put him to sleep. And I was right. He was out like a light.

I picked up his wrist. Running my nose along his forearm, I inhaled. He smelled sweet, like a child. He couldn't be more than seventeen. And he wouldn't remember a bit of this. He would recall the walk by the beach, but after that, his memory would fade into nothing.

I sank my teeth into his arm and sucked. Warm, sweet blood filled my mouth and in his sleep, Jason moaned. I couldn't help but smile. It was a sexual experience for mortals when I drank their blood. I figured it was the least I could do for them.

I swallowed and then drank more, enjoying the taste, the warmth and the texture. I hated that I liked it, but I did. The curse made my body crave it. However, what I enjoyed the most was the strength that I felt returning to my limbs. I knew that mouthful by mouthful, my color was returning. After I few minutes, I was full. I gently laid Jason's arm across his stomach and wiped my mouth.

His face was innocent and peaceful as he slept blissfully unaware. If I had to guess, I would guess that the experience had simply given him an erotic dream. And when he woke, he would only remember those sensations. Not the experience.

Sighing, I slipped out of the brush and back onto the beach. Jason would wake in a while and he would be perfectly fine, so I attempted to assuage my eternal guilt. I had only done what I had to do to survive. Like always.

As I walked, I noted the strength returning in my legs. I felt so much better now. I always put this off as long as I could. I allowed my energy to dip too low because I hated doing it. But it was done now for a while and I could bask in the afterglow.

I skirted around the bonfire and the partygoers and was just slipping into the shadows when someone called my name. I startled. There was no way that Jason was awake yet and I hadn't even told him my name.

I spun, only to find Brennan striding toward me. Apparently, he'd been at this party and I hadn't even seen him. The moonlight bathed him in ethereal light and I sucked in my breath. He was as handsome as I remembered.

"It's you," he breathed when he was two steps away. I was speechless. For the first time in a very long time, I didn't know what to say.

But it turned out that words weren't necessary. He stopped in front of me and before I could even react, he pulled me to him and his mouth came down upon my own, strong and soft at once.

Electricity jolted through me, snapping through my fingertips and toes, and stiffening my spine. I wanted to melt into this man, this boy... but I knew if I succumbed, he was done. He was giving me the most gentle, sensual kiss I had ever experienced and I found that I never wanted it to end.

But I ended it. Pulling away, I breathed raggedly as I tried to pull myself together. He reached out for me, but I stepped back. He couldn't touch me right now. His life depended on it.

"What the hell is going on?" he asked, his eyes slightly glazed. "Ever since the hospital, I've seen you in my mind. I want to be near you...I have this driving need to kiss you...and I had no way to find you. When you touch me... do you feel that?"

My eyes flew to his and found them to be full of confusion, desire and torment. He had only just met me and I was already torturing him. It was unfair.

"Do you?" he asked again, reaching for me once more. "Do you feel it too?"

I moved away, farther this time and stared at him hesitantly.

"Yes," I admitted.  And then I took off running.

# Chapter Three

"Wait!" Brennan called from behind me, but I didn't stop.

I flew as fast as I could while still appearing mortal. If I wanted, I could literally blur into motion, but that would give me away as being something other than a normal human, so I stretched my legs out in long strides and ran normally instead.

The beach sand made it difficult to run, though, and before I knew it, he had reached me, grabbing my hand.

"Stop," he insisted, electricity shooting through my forearm at his touch. I yanked my hand away.

"What is going on?" he asked. "I know you feel it, too. And I've never felt anything like it."

"Me neither," I admitted, but he stared at me doubtfully.

"Really? Because there is something about you... something different."

The moonlight reflected from his hazel eyes, making them seem golden. I found that I longed to reach out and touch him. When I said that I had never experienced such a feeling before, I hadn't lied. I felt drawn to him in a very strange way.

"Can we just go somewhere and talk?" he asked, his brow furrowed. "I won't touch you, I promise."

I fought the urge to laugh. Did he think I was scared for myself?

"What's funny?" he asked, his brow furrowed suspiciously.

"Nothing," I assured him. "It's not funny. I'm just… not afraid of you."

"And why would you be?" he asked calmly. "I won't hurt you. I just want to figure this out. I'm confused."

I always had a hard time classifying his age group. They were so close to manhood, but still possessed the innocence of boys. He was man-sized, built like a man and had the face of a man but his expression was slightly vulnerable and sweet, like a boy. As I stared at him while he stood uncertainly in the moonlight, something inside of me crumbled, like a wall falling down. I couldn't help it. I nodded.

"Okay," I whispered. "We can talk. I live near here."

Without waiting to see if he would follow me, because I was certain that he would, I turned and walked quickly towards my cottage. I heard his soft footsteps behind me and almost sighed, although I wasn't sure if it was from relief or disappointment.

Something pulled me to him, something invisible but inexplicable. It was there. And something that I had learned long ago was that just because you didn't understand something, didn't make it less real.

Climbing the stairs, I still felt him behind me. I had a feeling I would be able to sense his presence anywhere. It was like an electrical field next to me, a magnet drawing me to him. If there was ever a time when I needed my mother's advice, it was right now. She always knew everything. Surely she could explain this.

Unlocking the door, I switched on a lamp inside, illuminating the room with a soft glow.

"Please," I gestured him forward. "Come in."

Brennan stepped inside and looked around. "Nice place. Do you live here alone?"

I knew he was probably wondering how I paid for it. At the oldest, I looked like a college student. Glancing around, I did realize that it looked posh. Expensive furniture and rich woods, paired with modern touches like metal and glass made it chic and trendy. But I didn't have anything to do with the fashionable décor. It had come to me fully furnished. I simply had to make a rent payment every month. And that was easy to do when you were the daughter of the goddess of witchcraft. Conjuring things, like money, was child's play.

I nodded. "Yes, I live here alone."

There was a brief flash of relief on his face and I realized that he had been asking for another reason: To see if I had a boyfriend. For a reason I couldn't explain, that knowledge filled me with joy and caused my heart to flutter.

"Please, have a seat.  Get comfortable," I encouraged him, motioning toward the soft leather couch.  He settled onto one end and I sat on the faraway opposite end, perched nervously on the edge.

"How old are you?" I murmured.  He glanced at me, amusement apparent on his handsome face.

"Why do you ask?" he teased.  He certainly didn't have Jason's shyness issue.  Brennan seemed at home with anyone and he wasn't intimidated by me.

"Just curious," I answered with a shrug.

"No specific reason?" he raised an eyebrow.  I fought the urge to say, *Yes, because I'm 1,000 years old and I want to see exactly how much I might be robbing the cradle*.  But of course I didn't.

And robbing the cradle? I suddenly had the urge to do a face plant into my palms.   Robbing the cradle would imply that I had plans to seek a relationship with him. And I didn't.  Did I?

*Did I?*

I shook my head.  "Nope.  No specific reason."

"If you say so," he grinned.   "I'm eighteen, if you're still curious.  I go to college in town."

Long pause.

"And you?" he finally prompted.  "Now would be the time when you shared a little something about you."

"Oh." I looked at him blankly, observing the way his t-shirt stretched across his muscled chest.  I hadn't actually had a conversation with a mortal in a while and certainly not in this context. I wasn't sure what to say and fiddled with my fingers nervously.

"So, where are you from?" he prompted with a grin. "How old are you? Do you have a boyfriend?"

I glanced at him sharply and he laughed. I had forgotten how appealing his laugh was. It was impossibly smooth yet husky at the same time. I swallowed hard.

"Sorry," he chuckled. "I had to throw that last one in there." He was sprawled on his end of the couch, perfectly at ease with his arm stretched along the back.

I consciously forced myself to relax. I was being stupid. There was no reason to be nervous. After taking a deep breath and then another, I smiled.

"I'm eighteen, too," I answered. And I did look eighteen. "I'm not from here and no, I do not have a boyfriend."

"Well, now we're getting somewhere," Brennan grinned. He smile was beautiful and every time he smiled, it threatened to bowl me over at the knees. He was the epitome of the term 'golden boy'. Golden hair, butterscotch eyes, tanned skin. And I was sure that he was athletic. You could just tell.

"Do you play football?" I asked conversationally, remembering my social skills. He nodded.

"I do. Linebacker. But we're skirting the issue."

"The issue?"

He scooted down the couch toward me and I lunged to my feet, backing away.

"Why are you running from me?" he asked, his eye growing serious. As they did, their color shifted from butterscotch back to hazel. Odd. It seemed they reflected his mood. But that wasn't possible. Was it?

"I'm not running from you."

"Yes, you are," he said quietly, as he stood. His tall frame cast a long shadow against the wall and my gaze flickered toward it and then back to his face.

"Have I offended you somehow?" Brennan asked seriously. "Because I didn't mean to."

"No, of course not," I answered weakly.

My knees suddenly felt weak at his close proximity and I ached to have his hands lift up and touch me. I could practically feel the warmth emanating from him and I wanted to lean into it, into the palms of his masculine hands. My body almost moved toward him subconsciously and I had to fight to remain still.

*What was wrong with me?*

"Why am I so drawn to you?" he asked curiously, taking another step toward me, his question telling me that he was feeling the same.

And this time, when he approached, I didn't move away. I couldn't. I couldn't find the strength inside of me to step away from him. I clenched my fists at my sides and stood firm. I was not weak. I could do this. I wouldn't hurt him.

"I don't know," I admitted. My palms were growing clammy from my efforts, but I couldn't relax.

"But you feel it too," he observed, his eyes flitting to my fists. I was sure my knuckles were white from being gripped so tightly.

"Yes," I whispered.

He took a final step and lowered his head, covering my mouth with his. Colors exploded behind my closed eyelids and sensations that I couldn't even describe filled me up. My knees almost buckled and my heart throbbed, almost painfully, against my sternum. I wanted him. With everything in me, I wanted him.

But it was more than that. As his large hands splayed across my back, pulling me closer to him as he deepened the kiss, it was as if he completed me. He was something that I hadn't even realized was missing, but now that he was here, I never wanted to let go of him. It felt silly to even think something like that, but it was true.

I also felt an unbelievably strong inclination to take his soul. I wanted to consume it, inhale it and keep it inside of me. That startling desire pulled against my need to be near him and I fought to overcome the dangerous thoughts. *I could do this. I wouldn't hurt him.*

Wrapping my arms around his neck, I pulled him closer. It would be so easy. All I had to do was inhale. It was as easy as breathing. And I so, so wanted to. My chest practically ached from the urge.

But with an inner strength that I didn't even know that I possessed, I held my breath and loosened my arms. His tongue was in my mouth, his heart beating loudly against my chest. And with a start, I realized that our heart beats had synchronized. They were beating together. I could feel my pulse in my ears, roaring like a crashing waterfall.

Being with him felt so good, better than anything ever had in my entire life.

He finally pulled away, breathing raggedly.

"What was that?" he asked hoarsely.

I fought to regain my composure and walked away from him to the windows, where I stood in the light of the moon. It would strengthen me and by the gods, I needed strength right now.

He stared at me for the longest while, silently appraising me.

"You're beautiful, you know," he said softly. "But that's not it. That's not the reason that I need you."

"Probably not," I confirmed. "There's a lot about me that you don't know."

"I don't know anything about you," he laughed, breaking the tension. "I know that you're eighteen, you live alone and you don't have a boyfriend."

"Aren't those the important things?" I replied, leveling my gaze at him.

He nodded seriously. "Yes. But there's more to you- a lot more. Will you share it?"

"Maybe someday," I murmured. I strangely found that I really did want to. I wanted to share everything about me with this boy who I had just met. It made no sense. I had lived for a thousand years without once feeling this way.

Brennan studied me again, but made no move toward me. It was as though he understood that I needed space. I wanted him near, but I didn't know if I could restrain myself.

"Touch my hand," he requested, holding it out. "I want to see if it happens again."

Sighing, I crossed the room once more and stood in front of him. Reaching trembling fingers out, I touched mine to his, as my eyes met his.

The same strong sensations flooded me, like every natural source of light in the universe was entering my body. He grasped my hand and pulled me to him, bending to kiss me fiercely once more.

"I almost can't stand it," he growled against my lips. "I can't seem to get close enough to you."

I knew the feeling. I was clutching his back, trying to pull him against me as close as I could. And it wasn't enough.

"Tell me about you," he said softly. "Please."

He released me, but held my hand. And I was grateful for it. I felt almost panicky at the thought of being separated from him and I found that as each minute passed, I was more and more able to withstand the temptation to drink his soul.

"Let's walk," I suggested, pulling him toward the door.

I hesitated in the door frame to allow him to pass, but as his large, warm body slid past mine, he paused and dipped his head to kiss me again. His lips were warm and soft against mine and I knew that I would never get enough of him. The moonlight bathed him in silver, illuminating the face that I knew would haunt me from this day forward.

"I can't keep away from you," he said with a smile as he pulled away. "I can't explain it."

I said nothing, but smiled slightly as we walked down the wooden steps for the beach. My mind was turning a mile a minute, trying to decide what to say, how much to explain. Then I frantically wondered why I was even considering it. I really didn't know anything about this man. But my body seemed to think otherwise.

"Tell me more about you," I said as we stepped onto the soft sand of the beach. "Tell me everything."

He grinned and I sucked in my breath. The moonlight made him seem other-worldly. His scent wafted toward me on the breeze and I inhaled, breathing in the male scent. He smelled delicious.

"Everything?" he asked smiling. "I don't want to bore you."

"And you won't," I assured him. "I want to know everything about you."

He started talking and I allowed myself to become immersed in the sexiness of his voice. His words blended together as he told me of his childhood, his upbringing, his parents. He had lived in this area his whole life, his mother had died years ago with cancer and he had no brothers or sisters. I found nothing in his words to explain my connection to him.

Yet, as he finished speaking, he brushed his hand across my lower back to guide me around a piece of driftwood in our path and the strange electricity followed his touch and flickered up my spine. There was certainly something between us.

"Now, you," he prodded. "Tell me everything."

I sighed. "I wish I could," I told him honestly. "But there are things about me that you couldn't possibly understand and I wouldn't want you to. I don't want you to see me in that light."

He looked puzzled. "In what light? You don't want me to know the truth?"

I studied his face for a moment. "Honestly, I would like nothing more," I admitted cautiously. "But for the first time in my life, I'm afraid. I'm afraid that once you know everything, you won't want anything to do with me. I need to figure out how to explain. Can you trust me for a while? I know you don't know me. But just give me a while to sort this out. Can you?"

He nodded slowly. "Yes. I can."

I hadn't even realized I had been holding my breath but when he spoke, I breathed again. The tension I had been holding exhaled with my breath.

He reached over and grasped my hand. "It's getting late," he said softly. "Let me walk you back to your house."

I nodded and we turned back, walking along the edge of the water as we returned to my little cottage.

The air was crisp and the breeze coming off of the lake was cold, so he wrapped his arm around my shoulders.

I melted into his warmth and strength. I instinctively knew that I was meant to be here. Right here. There was no other place for me to be. I fit into the crook of his shoulder perfectly. We fell into comfortable silence as we walked and I drifted into deep thought.

I remembered a story once that my mother had told me. She had been talking about my father, Mormo. No one could understand why she loved him and she had been trying to explain why.

*"There was a time, Empusa,"* she had said, *"When Zeus was so worried about others overthrowing his throne that he took some drastic measures. He had overthrown his own parents for the throne, you know. So, he split every soul into two and cast them into the universe. That way, everyone - mortal and god alike- would be driven to find their other half, rather than focused on taking his crown."*

Soul mates. Could that be the thing that was pulling Brennan and I together like magnets? Could that be the reason why I was able to resist drinking his soul even when he kissed me as passionately as he did? Did something, deep down inside of me, recognize that he was already mine?

I glanced at him. He was walking beside me silently, as lost in thought as I was, but his arm was still firmly draped around my shoulders as though it belonged there. He felt it too. I knew that. I didn't want him to leave me, not even to go home for the night. How else could I explain that except that he might be my soul mate?

It had certainly been true for my mother. There was no other feasible reason why she would be so attached to my heinous father after all that he had become and had done through the years.

"A penny for your thoughts," Brennan offered as we stepped up the first step to my house.

"They're worth a lot more than that," I deflected.

"I imagine that they are," he answered. "Can I call you tomorrow?"

I nodded and gave him my phone number, my eyes frozen on his.

"You have very unusual eyes," he told me as he moved closer. "I've never seen gray eyes before. They're beautiful."

"Thank you," I answered, leaning into him once more with a sigh.

He groaned and kissed me again, crushing me softly to his chest. He kissed me as though he'd never see me again and I clung to him as though I believed that, too. But the thought of that scared me, which scared me even more. I couldn't allow someone to get close to me, someone that my father could hurt. But I was terrified at the thought of letting Brennan go.

I finally pulled away, shoving my hair behind my ears with shaking hands.

"I'll talk to you tomorrow," I said before I leaned up and kissed him lightly one more time. Then once more. I couldn't seem to keep away from him.

He chuckled, a low husky sound in the night.

"I will most definitely call you tomorrow."

He squeezed my hand, one last jolt of energy flooding through me, before he turned and strode down the wooden steps. I watched him until he disappeared into the night before going inside and closing the door.

I felt the separation immediately and I didn't enjoy it. It was cold and empty. I wanted, *needed* him to come back. I immediately berated myself. I had only just met him. He was a mortal. There was no earthly reason that I should be so attracted to him. But the answer, I knew, wasn't an earthly answer so logic was no longer a factor.

Wearily, I stripped off my clothes and pulled a nightgown on, dropping into the cool sheets of my bed. Listening to the crashing waves of the lake, I stared at my moonstone glistening in the moonlight until I finally allowed my eyes to close.

My mother was waiting for me.

She stood proudly in my dream with red lips and blonde curls hanging to the small of her back. She didn't look anything like what you would imagine the goddess of witchcraft to look like. She was very beautiful and young. Appearances were deceiving, however. She was ancient. She might possess an ethereal, delicate beauty, but she was oh-so-powerful. She could crumple the moon from the sky if she wished.

"Empusa," she admonished. "Tell me where you are. There are things going on now that you don't understand. I sense them. I've seen you in visions."

"Mother," I answered calmly. "I'm not going to the Underworld. I've told you a thousand times. I do not trust Hades, even if you do."

She shook her head impatiently.

"It's not that I trust him," she muttered. "It's that he made a deal in front of every Olympian. He has to uphold it, don't you understand? If we stand in front of him, he will release you from your curse. The second he does, he will send out search parties for your father and bring Mormo to the Underworld. You will be safe forever."

"No one is safe forever," I answered tiredly. "But tell me, what of these visions? What did you see?"

"I can't be certain," she answered, clearly unhappy with that. She was not used to imperfect clarity. Her magic was flawless, her prophecies perfect. "I cannot see for sure. But look."

She waved an elegant hand and a scattered array of visions appeared before me. I saw myself standing in the moonlight by the lake, I saw myself talking with Daniel Delacorte in the hospital, reading him a mystery novel and smiling at him and I even saw Gaia. She was sitting in the chair in my bedroom as I slept. I'd have to talk with her about that. It was slightly creepy.

But then there was Brennan. Handsome and strong, he moved to the front of the visions. Only he wasn't himself. He was shining with the light of the sun, armed in bronzed armor and gleaming eyes. And then I realized that it wasn't actually Brennan at all. It was someone who looked very, very much like him.

"What the…." I whispered. My mother nodded.

"Exactly," she answered. "What is going on? Wherever you are, what are you doing? Why are you with Apollo's son?"

# Chapter Four

"What the hell do you mean, Apollo's son?" I demanded. "Brennan isn't Apollo's son. He's mortal!"

My mother sighed, twisting her lovely, youthful features into a slightly impatient scowl as she faced me.

"Empusa," she admonished. "You should know by now that not everything is what it seems. I assure you, Brennan is most certainly Apollo's son."

"But that's impossible," I whispered, picturing the innocence on Brennan's handsome face. "He's not a god."

"No, he isn't. He's a demi-god, like you," my mother agreed. "And to be honest, I doubt he even knows it."

"How the hell is that even possible?" I screeched. "How can someone be a demi-god and not know it?"

My mother leveled a gaze at me and glared. "Watch your mouth, Empusa. There is no need to swear like a sailor. It's possible because if he was born as a mortal, how *would* he know? He obviously would think he was mortal."

I stared at her in confusion and she sighed once again, apparently trying to figure out how to explain something complex to a child. I glared back at her. This didn't make any sense at all and I was a pretty bright person.

"Empusa, you know that the Olympians were trapped in the Underworld for several thousand years," she began patiently. I nodded. I had been there in the not so distant past when they had been freed by Harmonia, the goddess of peace.

"Well, during that time, Hades sought to keep them content and pleased," she continued. "Several of the Olympians have… what we might call… a penchant for mortal women. So, Hades had mortal women brought to them. Then afterward, he would take the memories of those women and return them home. The mortals never even remembered what happened to them. Probability would suggest that at least some of them became pregnant."

"And they wouldn't have known who the father was," I whispered, finally comprehending. "So, Brennan's mother thought that her husband was the father of her baby. Brennan has no idea…"

"He has no idea that he is the son of a god," my mother confirmed, nodding her head, satisfied that I finally understood. "But he is, in fact, a mortal, too. Unless Zeus decrees otherwise, he will eventually die like a mortal."

I knew that much was true and that realization ran through me like a knife. I would lose him eventually. Mortality had never been an issue for me since I was the daughter of two immortals. I was born immortal.

*But Brennan was not.*

"Also, Empusa," my mother continued, bringing my attention back to her. "You need to keep something in mind. The energy of two demi's is more powerful and more noticeable then the energy of just one. You will make it easier for your father to find you if you continue to consort with this boy."

I looked at her. *Consort?* That made it sound so seedy.

"Your combined energy would be something to see, though," she mused. "Think of it, Empusa. The daughter of the goddess of the moon and the son of the god of the sun. Your energy would be exquisite and quite powerful."

I thought about the connection that Brennan and I shared, the jolting, powerful sensations. Could that be the cause? Because we were polar-opposites?

"Mother, something strange happens when we touch. I feel oddly connected to him and him to me. It's very odd and I've never experienced such a thing. Is that because of our parents?"

She studied me calmly, her beautiful blue eyes full of ancient wisdom. "Tell me more, my sweet."

So, I relayed everything that had happened from the time that Brennan and I had met. Every strange sensation, every electrical jolt, the strange attraction. The fact that I had not accidentally killed him even when I stayed in his embrace longer than I should have.  When I was finished, she stared thoughtfully at me for a while before she finally spoke.

"I think it's likely a combination of everything.  You didn't kill him because he is a demi.  He can certainly die, don't mistake that.  But he is more resistant to you than a mere mortal.  This attraction, though, it is interesting.  I would say… and I am guessing… but I would say that you might be soul mates.  If that is true, then you have found your other half.  I only pray that he is a good match for you."

She paused, a long pregnant pause and I swallowed hard.  I had wondered that very thing.

"Is he?" she asked, her face betraying her worry.

"Is he what?" I asked absently, my thoughts still focused on Brennan, on the very real idea that he actually might belong to me.

"If he does turn out to be your soul mate, is he a good match for you?"

That was a very good question.

"I don't know," I admitted.  "I only just met him.  But he seems kind and good."

"As you know, Empusa," she cautioned.  "Things are not always what they seem."

"You're the goddess of witchcraft," I snapped back impatiently.  "Can't you see something about this in a vision?  It's important."

Soul Kissed

"I realize that it is important," she sighed. "Empusa, you must learn patience. I am not all-knowing or all-seeing. This is one of those things that will be revealed to you in due time, I'm afraid. Until then, use caution. The only thing we are certain of is that Brennan is Apollo's son."

"But Apollo is a decent god," I mused. "He's kind, right?"

My mother laughed. "Most of the Olympians *can* be kind, but every one of them can be ruthless, as well. Some more than others. Apollo is a kind person, true. He's a free spirit and he's very handsome. He has a weakness for mortal women and even a few men. His passion doesn't discriminate between the sexes. Remember this, though, while Brennan will have his father's DNA and might have some of Apollo's tendencies, his personality will have been shaped by his mortal parents. Personality is more learned than inherited."

"What about his gifts?" I asked hesitantly. "I saw his eyes change color with his mood."

"Of course he will have abilities," she confirmed. "Many of which he probably isn't even aware of. Mortals tend to block out or ignore the things that they don't understand."

I nodded. "So what should I do?"

"You should tell me where you are so that I can come to you," she urged. "Please, Empusa. Now more than ever, you need me. This could be more dangerous now than we even thought."

"No!" I snapped. "Mother, I love you. But you cannot come here. I cannot take the risk."

"But it appears that you are already taking risks," she argued. "It's better to do that with me there to help. Especially if you and Brennan do turn out to be connected. You know, moonlight does not exist on its own. Do you realize that? Moonlight is simply a reflection of the light of the sun. Think about that. What implications do you think that holds for you, little moon princess, if you are tied to Brennan? His father is the god of the sun! Tell me where you are. We'll sort this out together."

"No."

We stared at each other, our gazes unwavering. Finally, she smiled. "I see that you inherited your determination from me. That pleases me at the same time that it pains me. I love you, Empusa. I won't stop looking for you."

I opened my eyes.

Morning light flooded my bedroom and I yawned. I had been dream-walking all night, which left me tired. Dream-walking was not conducive to a good night's sleep.

"It's about time you woke," Gaia grumbled from the chair in the corner. I sat up, rubbing my eyes and then stared at her.

"Gaia, how often do you sit in here while I sleep? It's slightly unnerving."

She laughed, unaffected by my comment. "You talk in your sleep, moon princess. It is entertaining. You've been talking to your mother all morning. Did she come to you again?"

I nodded, staring absently out the window at the magnificent view of the lake. The morning sun was reflecting from the surface, creating beautiful prisms of light. The sight of the sun's glory reminded me that Brennan was the son of Apollo. And that was something that I didn't wish to share with Gaia just yet. I wasn't sure why, but I wanted to keep it to myself for the time being.

"Well, what did she say? You were agitated while you were sleeping."

"Same old, same old," I replied. "She wanted me to tell her where I was."

Gaia sniffed. "I can guess how that conversation ended."

She kept talking but I tuned her out as I watched the frigid water lap at the shore. It was soothing, rhythmic and mesmerizing. The foamy froth slid over the sand and pebbles to touch the shore, only to be sucked back into the lake, time and time again. Leaning forward, I cracked open the window, allowing the chilly Autumn breeze to fill my room. Tucking my feet beneath me, I continued to observe the beautiful scene outdoors, while pretending to listen to my ghostly friend.

"You're not even listening to me," she complained, glaring at me as she noticed. Since my back was to her, I didn't see her glare, but I felt its impact in between my shoulder blades.

"Of course I am," I replied, not turning around. "You're talking about my mother."

"Yes. What did I say about her?"

I drew a blank. I had no idea. But a movement from the staircase leading to my house captured my attention and I gasped.

Brennan was climbing the stairs, breathtakingly beautiful in the morning light, wearing a pair of well-fitting jeans and a v-necked black shirt that hugged his chest. Appropriately, being in the sun agreed with him. He looked glorious as the sunlight seemed to reflect off of every angle of his face. He held two foam cups in his hands. The breath constricted in my throat and all I could do was point.

"What is it?" Gaia asked in concern as she flitted to the window to look. "Ahhh. Your boyfriend." She turned to look at me. "You'd better get up. You're not even dressed."

She was right.

I flew out of bed in a blur and threw open my closet doors.

"You're never going to have enough time," she pointed out. "He's almost to the door."

She was right again. I glanced at myself in the mirror. My hair was disheveled, my nightgown barely covered my butt and I hadn't even brushed my teeth yet. Good lord.

A firm knock on my door resounded through the small house.

"I told you," Gaia smirked.

"Go on- leave," I instructed. "You don't get to eavesdrop."

Glaring at me, she faded into invisibility. I could only hope she was gone because I never quite knew.

I tucked my hair behind my ears and drew in a deep breath before I walked to the door in my nightgown. I opened it and Brennan smiled, his gaze drifting over me and then back up to my face, keeping it there. I had to give him credit for that.

"Good morning, sunshine," he grinned. "I owed you a coffee." He held one of the cups out and I took it, careful not to touch his hand. It was too early in the morning for spine-tingling electricity.

"I'm sorry. I'm not dressed yet," I pointed out the obvious. "If you want to come in, I'll throw some clothes on really quick."

"Oh, don't get dressed on my account," he grinned again and I smiled back. He had an ornery sense of humor and I found that I liked it. He dropped lazily onto my sofa, sipping at his coffee, making a show of being patient. "But if you must, I'll be right here."

I nodded and spun back around for my bedroom, making sure to close the door tightly behind me. I leaned against it for a moment, gathering my composure. My potential soul mate was lounging in my living room. And he just happened to be the son of

Apollo, the most handsome god who had ever lived. Heaven help me.

I threw some clothes on, yanked a brush through my hair, brushed my teeth and was ready in five minutes flat.

Opening the door a crack, I peeked through. Brennan's hazel eyes were boring a hole into my own. I startled and he laughed, the warm sound enticing me to walk nearer to him. There was something about him, an easy way of being, that made it incredibly hard to resist him. He cocked an eyebrow.

"Well, are you dressed?"

I nodded, my fingers still curled around the door. "Yes."

"Then why are you hiding in your bedroom?"

I quickly straightened and threw the door open. "I don't hide. Not from you, anyway."

"Yet you just were." Again with the cocked eyebrow.

"If you raise your eyebrows any higher, they're going to embed into your hairline," I told him.

He laughed again. "You're funny," he observed. "Kind-of snarky. I like it. It suits you."

It was my turn to raise my eyebrows. "It suits me? And how would you know what suits me?"

He shrugged. "I wouldn't. But why don't you come out here and tell me more about you so that maybe I can get an idea?"

Shit. I had walked right into that and mentally slapped myself on the forehead.

I eyed him cautiously and then mentally slapped myself again. I wasn't afraid of anyone, much less a mortal boy. He wasn't a *mortal boy*, I reminded myself. But still. I wasn't intimidated by anyone, mortal or otherwise. I walked purposefully out to the living room and perched on the sofa on the opposite end from Brennan, trying to ignore the fact that my hands were shaking and my knees felt weak.

Brennan turned to me calmly, seeking out my gaze. He was cool and collected, so much so that his next question startled me.

"If I'm not a mortal boy, then what am I?" he inquired politely.

Holy shit. He had read my mind.

# Chapter Five

"You can read my mind," I stammered without thinking.

"So it would seem," Brennan answered, still calm. "Why is that? What is happening?"

My own mind was spinning. Of course, he could read it...because gods could read the minds of other gods. I was probably the first demi he had ever come into contact with, so I was the first mind he could read. I quickly hid my thoughts so that he couldn't hear them, camouflaging my hesitation with a question.

"Didn't you wonder about this strange ability last night?" I asked him, slightly accusatory.

"I didn't realize it until just now. It was a strange feeling and at first I thought that you had spoken out loud. But today, I was looking at your mouth and I knew that you hadn't spoken. *I read your mind*. And you're not surprised by that. Can you tell me why?"

For the first time, his voice was slightly tight, although his face was only a bit anxious. He was handling it well. Maybe too well.

"Why aren't you more upset by this?" I narrowed my eyes suspiciously.

"I don't know," he admitted. "I should be upset. I should be panicked right now. But instead, when I am next to you, I feel calm. Like all is right in the world. But now your mind is blank- I can't hear a thing. How are you doing that? Can you hear *my* thoughts?"

I paused. I probably could if I concentrated. I just hadn't known that he was a demi before so it hadn't occurred to me to try. And I couldn't admit that because then I would have to explain his true lineage. How much should I tell him? But in my uncertainty, I forgot to veil my silent question.

"Tell me everything," he growled. "Not just the parts that you want me to hear. Something is going on here, something big. And I want to know about it."

"There's nothing 'going on,'" I answered with a sigh. "At least, nothing that hasn't been 'going on' for a very long time. It's just life, Brennan."

"But there's more to life than I know about," he prompted. I nodded reluctantly, pushing away the image of my mother's warnings. He could read my mind. He deserved some sort of explanation.

"Yes," I replied simply. "There is. But let's not talk about it here. Let's go outdoors." Neutral territory just seemed the way to go, for some reason.

He nodded. "I have a picnic in my car. My plan was to invite you to a picnic on the beach. I know a great place, but we'll need to drive there."

"Alright," I agreed. I guess I agreed too quickly, because he looked at me slightly suspiciously.

"And you'll tell me what I need to know?"

"I'll tell you what you need to know."

He looked satisfied with that as he stood, shoving a long hand into his pocket. He was really, really big. I craned my neck as I stared up at him.

"How tall are you?"

He smirked as he looked down at me. "6'5". How tall are you, shortcake?"

I glared up at him. "I only seem short next to you, because you're a giant. I'm 5'7", which is perfectly tall for a female."

I reached past him to pick up my favorite gray cashmere shawl from the arm of the couch, but as I curled my arm around him, he grabbed my fingers. Electricity shot up my arm, branching into my shoulder and down my spine. I stiffened for a moment and then hardened myself against the overwhelming sensations. I was going to have to learn to deal with it without feeling weak- a challenging task.

Brennan closed his eyes for a scant moment, sliding his fingers up to my elbow and back down to my wrist, a whisper soft touch that left a tingling trail behind it. He opened his eyes back up and stared into mine.

"Why does it feel almost orgasmic to touch you?"

I stayed quiet. But he was right. It was almost orgasmic. Picking up my shawl, he wrapped it around my shoulders and then lifted my chin with one finger. He kissed my lips, gently and briefly.

"That's how I really wanted to say good morning," he admitted, pulling me to him. The length of his body was long and hard against mine and I found that I wanted to stand here forever, just like this. Leaning forward, I rested my forehead against his chest, feeling the beat of his heart.

*What was wrong with me?* This was not like me at all. I didn't need anything or anybody. But I literally felt as though moving away from him would possibly cause me pain. Physical pain and definitely some mental anguish.

Lifting my face, I whispered, "I'll tell you everything."

"Wasn't that already the plan?" he asked softly, tucking a tendril of loose hair behind my ear. I found that I wanted to lean into his hand, but restrained myself. I really, really hated appearing weak.

I nodded. I didn't bother to tell him that I hadn't really planned on telling him everything. But now I found that I wanted to, regardless of the consequences. The only way we would get to the bottom of whatever was between us was surely to have complete honesty- a concept that was fairly foreign to me in my current on-the-lam situation.

Gathering every ounce of strength within me, I pulled away from Brennan and stepped out of his radius of warmth. The separation instantly made me feel chilled.

"Okay. Where are we going?" I asked shakily as I grabbed my purse.

"It's a surprise," he answered.  He sounded stronger than I felt.

Striding past me, he held the door for me – a perfect gentleman.  Although he wasn't touching me, his eyes were locked with mine in a gaze as intimate as a caress.

"Thank you," I murmured, trying not to inhale as I passed him.  I wasn't exactly sure how far I could trust myself just yet.  I wanted to make sure that his soul stayed right where it belonged- inside of his body.

We stepped out into the morning light and quickly walked down the wooden steps that led to my house. The beach was serene this morning, without another soul in sight.  The water lapped quietly at the shore, the sea gulls flying in circles overhead.  Their cries were the only thing interrupting the silence of the scene surrounding us.

"So, we have to drive to your picnic spot?" I asked curiously as we walked.  He nodded.

"Mm-hmm.  Do you want to know why?"

I didn't answer, but stared at him expectantly.

"I'll take that as a yes," he said wryly.  "We have to drive there because it's the best picnic spot in Michigan, maybe even in the world."

"So, you like to exaggerate," I observed.  "Good to know."

He laughed.  "I'm serious.  I'm sure you've heard of the Harbor Pointe Hotel. It burned to the ground in the

1920's, but the ruins are still there on the edge of the lake. People say it's haunted. I don't know about that, but it definitely has an intriguing quality about it."

Oh, perfect. A haunted ruins. Just perfect for a girl who could see ghosts. I quickly suppressed my thoughts and my hesitation, offering him a smile instead.

"Sounds great," I assured him.

Brennan turned to me and held out his hand, his eyes meeting mine as if it was almost a challenge. I met his gaze and placed my hand in his tanned fingers, soaking in the instant jolting sensations. The more we touched, the more I grew accustomed to it.

And liked it. It was something special and specific to us. It was something that only we shared.

I gulped hard as we continued toward his car- a large black Land Rover type thing. It had big lights on top, large tires and tinted windows. I paused.

"That's yours?"

He grinned. "Yep. Are you afraid?"

I nodded. "Very."

"I thought you were never afraid- at least of me?"

I shook my head. "No, I said that I wouldn't hide from you. There's a difference."

He laughed, a husky rich sound that instantly turned my blood warm and made me ache to reach out for him and draw him to me. I pulled away from him, wrapping my arms around my waist instead. He looked at me, puzzled.

"What's wrong?"

"Nothing," I answered. "It's not you."

"It's not you, it's me?" he asked. "I'm getting a break-up line already?" His handsome face was puzzled. I shook my head.

"No, of course not. Not yet anyway. There has to be a relationship of some sort to constitute a break-up. And there's nothing between us."

He sought out my gaze. "Nothing?" His tone was assured because he knew otherwise.

I looked away. There was no need to carry on this conversation. He and I both knew that something was there. There was no need to try and classify it.

He opened the door to his monstrous vehicle and I climbed inside, buckling up. Within minutes, we were cruising along the highway next to the water and I stared outside. The rugged shoreline passed in a blur through my window. And Brennan was right. It didn't take long to get there.

Before I knew it, we were climbing back out again in a sandy parking lot. I planted my feet and looked around.

"I don't see any ruins," I observed. All I could see was an empty beach and the lake. A beautiful view, but no ruins.

He chuckled. "We have to walk a little ways."

He had a picnic basket in his hand and I gulped. I was sure that he hadn't packed what I needed to eat. Mortals tended to frown on blood-drinking. Just thinking about that part of my secret made my heart pound erratically in my chest and Brennan turned to me, his expression puzzled.

"What's wrong?" he asked curiously, concern evident in his voice.

"Nothing," I quickly assured him. "Why do you ask?"

"Because I can feel that something is wrong. I can't explain it, so don't ask me to. But I can feel that you are upset... or nervous... or scared. Or something."

He searched my face. "What is it?"

"Nothing," I replied limply. "There's just a lot about me that you don't know."

"But I'd like to," he answered softly. "Anything that you want to tell me, I want to hear."

"I doubt that," I muttered. He turned back to me, his face set determinedly.

"Don't," he said. "Don't doubt it. There's nothing you can say to me that will scare me away."

"Again, I doubt that," I replied. "If you knew everything there was to know about me, you would run away and hide." I chewed my lip for a second as I thought. "You know," I mused, "That might not be a bad idea. Over lunch, I'll tell you everything."

He raised an eyebrow. "You want me to run away and never see you again?"

I sighed. "No. But I don't want you to get hurt. Being near me—it could get you hurt."

He looked at me doubtfully as we walked. "Oh, really? By whom?"

"By any number of people," I snapped. "But you can begin with me."

"You're going to hurt me?" he asked dubiously. "I have to tell you- my heart is a little tougher than that. Do your best."

Before I could think, before I could even breathe, I blurred into movement, plowing Brennan over and straddling him as I held him to the ground with goddess strength. He squirmed but couldn't move me and I made a mental note. He hadn't learned how to tap into his demi-god strength yet. I ignored his astonishment.

"Your heart isn't what I'm worried about," I answered softly as I dipped my head and ran my tongue along his bottom lip. As the connection between us practically snapped with electricity, I nipped at his lip lightly, then released my hold on his hands... opting to run my own against his sides lightly. I ached to inhale his soul and I clenched my jaw tightly to prevent it.

Brennan's breath caught in his throat and he hesitated, perfectly calm with his hands on my back. He didn't try to get away, he simply lay perfectly still. He remained calm as he gazed trustingly into my eyes.

"I'm not afraid," he replied. "So, again- give it your best."

"You don't want that, trust me," I whispered as I backed away from him, allowing him to sit up. I scrambled to my feet and offered him a hand. He took it and I pulled him to his feet.

"Maybe I do," he replied, his voice sexy in its huskiness. "Maybe I'm willing and able to take whatever you've got to give."

I stared at him in confusion. "Are we still talking about me scaring you?"

He laughed and the moment lightened.

Holding out his hand, he asked, "Shall we?"

I realized that we were standing at the foot of a sandy trail that seemed to lead into the trees that lined the bluffs, all of which hugged the shore. There was no one around us- not a single soul. If I walked back there with him, I could very well be putting his life at risk. Would I be able to control myself? It had been the very reason I had wanted to leave my house and go outdoors- to put a buffer between us.

"Well?" he raised an eyebrow. "I won't bite."

"But maybe *I* will," I muttered, as I put my hand within his.

"Promises, promises," he grinned. And I had to smile. His sense of humor was as contagious as his bright smile. He had most definitely inherited his father's legendary charm.

I focused on controlling myself as we followed the winding trail toward the edge of the bluffs. As I concentrated on my internal battle, the scenery around me blended together and my feet moved forward on autopilot. But I knew when we arrived. Besides the stillness and sense of hallowed ground that surrounded us, there were spirits everywhere.

Large stone blocks were scattered around us, half embedded in the ground. Partial walls stood here and there, with moss growing on them. The sand from the bluffs blew against the stones, drifting from the wind. Trees stood around us, all the way to the edge of the bluffs, which overlooked the water. It was a beautiful and haunting place.

And most certainly haunted.

A girl, incredibly pale, sat hunched over on a nearby stone. I tried not to make eye-contact, but inevitably, our eyes met. Hers widened and she lunged to her feet, her sheer dress fluttering around her as she clutched at her chest.

"You can see me!" she exclaimed, turning around to look at the other spirits. "She can see us!"

I tried to ignore her as she flitted to my side, her long hair flowing behind her.

"I know you can see me!" she cried, her fingers chillingly cold as she grasped my arm. She had learned to touch solid objects so she had been around for a while.

While Brennan's back was turned as he set up the picnic, I shook my head quickly at the ghost, trying to convey the message that she should leave me alone. But she didn't take the hint.

"How do we leave here?" she asked, a growing tone of desperation in her voice. "I just want to leave. Can you help us?"

I was puzzled. How were they trapped here? Traveling to the Underworld was easy after you died. The other spirits were converging upon me and I tried to tune out their cries and questions as Brennan turned back to me.

"Ready to eat?" he motioned at his picnic spread.

He had done well for a single guy, I had to admit. He had even brought a daisy in a little vase. It was hard to concentrate with the ghostly prattling of the spirits chattering around me, but I managed to tune them out by focusing with laser precision on Brennan's face. Pretending that I had blinders on, I stared directly into his eyes.

I nodded. "Yes. I'm starving."

Lucky for me, I could eat any kind of food that I wanted with no ill effect. But it wouldn't nourish me. Only mortal blood could do that.

Sinking onto the soft blanket that Brennan had spread onto the ground, I waited while he sat beside me and during the short pause, I wondered what to say to him. How much should I explain?

He turned and the sun shone down through a break in the tree-tops, shimmering through the gold tones in his hair. He was practically radiant and I could see why mortal women had found Apollo irresistible over the years. I swallowed hard.

"There is nothing I'd rather do than take you into my arms right now," he began, running one finger lightly along the inside of my forearm. "But I really need some answers right now and I have a feeling that you have them. Can we please talk?"

I swallowed again. I had to admire how calm he was. Putting myself into his shoes, I didn't think that I would be even half as collected as he was. I nodded.

"Yes," I murmured. "But I doubt you will like what I have to say."

"That's alright," he replied confidently. "It doesn't matter if I like it or not. The truth is always the best. Where would you like to start?"

Without waiting for me to reply, he slid his hand over mine. "How about here?"

"What do you mean?" I asked.

"Let's start with… why is there electricity between us?"

"Okay," I began. "That's actually the easiest part to explain. Let's see…" I pondered where to begin and just decided to jump in. Brennan's hazel eyes were glued to mine as he waited.

"Have you ever heard the theory about soul mates?" I asked. I had to give him credit- his mouth didn't even twitch as he shook his head, not even a tiny smile.

"No."

"Well, there is a theory that once upon a time, Zeus split everyone's souls into two in an effort to protect his throne. He figured that if everyone was preoccupied with finding their 'other half', that they wouldn't be concerned with trying to overtake his crown so his rule would be safe forever."

Brennan stared at me, waiting for me to say more. When I didn't, he continued slowly.

"Okay. So in the land of mythos, soul mates exist. But that doesn't explain why you and I feel what we do here in reality."

I studied him for a second, choosing my words carefully. "It does if mythos and reality are one and the same."

The ghosts surrounding us had fallen silent, each of them staring at Brennan as if waiting for his reaction. I waited with them for several long moments, each second passing more slowly than the previous. I suddenly realized that I was holding my breath and I exhaled slowly, the silence still smothering me.

Finally, Brennan broke the tension by throwing back his head and laughing.

I stared at him like he was an idiot.

"What is so funny?"

He was still chuckling as he replied. "You had me there for a second. I thought you were serious."

I narrowed my eyes, but remained silent. I focused on not shooting off a sharp retort. After all, he was only reacting the way any normal mortal would. He stopped laughing and appraised me silently for a second, looking at me carefully as though he was trying to determine my sanity level.

"Were you serious?" he asked hesitantly.

"As a heart attack," I replied through gritted teeth.

More silence.

I didn't break my gaze, instead keeping it locked on him.

"So," he finally murmured. "You think that you and I are soul mates."

I nodded. "I don't see any other explanation. And it isn't a far-fetched theory. The world isn't…. well, it isn't what you think it is. Mythology is real. It exists. I should know. I'm part of it. And so are you- you just don't know it."

"*I'm* a part of it?" He looked astonished, hesitant, leery… all rolled into one. I knew he was still trying to determine my sanity.

"I'm not crazy," I assured him. "Watch."

I pointed to a small, green bush nearby and murmured, "Fire."

The little bush immediately burst into flame, the orange fingers licking toward the sky. Brennan jumped and moved away from me, but still remained seated. His hazel eyes reflected the golds and reds of the fire as he watched the bush burn.

After a silent moment, he turned to me. "What are you?"

Amazingly, he still didn't seem afraid. He was taken aback, for certain, but not afraid. Or if he was, he was masking it very well.

"I'm the same as you," I answered quietly. "You just don't know it yet."

"Alright. Let me re-phrase. What are *we*?" He was growing impatient.

"Stay calm, okay?" I asked him, laying my hand over his own. "I'll tell you, but don't freak out."

He nodded and kept his hand beneath mine.

"You're a demi-god. Your father is Apollo, the god of the sun. Your mother didn't even know it. Her memory of your conception was taken away."

"A demi-god," Brennan repeated the words. "Which means that you're..."

"A demi-god." I nodded. "My mother is Hecate, the goddess of witchcraft."

Brennan shook his head wryly. "I don't believe this. I can't. This is unreal."

Before I could say another word, the moonstone on my bracelet began glowing, a soft ethereal glow against my skin. I sucked in air, unable to speak, my heart pounding in my chest like a drum. Around me, the ghosts began flitting to and fro.

"Your father," the girl who I had made eye contact with murmured. "Your father is coming."

"He's coming."

"He's coming."

All of the ghosts were murmuring and each of them sounded afraid. Suddenly, Gaia appeared out of nowhere, her face drawn and anxious.

"Empusa," she cried. "He's here."

And then suddenly he was.

In a swirling fog of mist, Mormo stepped from thin air. His black cloak fluttered in the wind and his eyes, as gray as mine, glittered in the sun. He was pale and dark-haired, like me. But his face was as solemn as death. He took one step toward me and I grasped Brennan's hand.

"Away," I gasped.
And we were gone.

# Chapter Six

We emerged onto the deserted fairways of Adventureland Amusement Park as fear coursed through my veins like ice water. Since it was October, the park had closed for the winter so the normally bustling walkways were silent and still. The only things moving were the dead leaves blowing across the pavement. The only sound was my pounding heart.

"What the hell?" Brennan demanded as he turned to me. "What the hell just happened? Why are we were? How did we get here?"

I spun in a circle, checking our perimeter. If Mormo had been close enough to us when we left, he could have followed us here. But I realized as I examined our surroundings that had apparently not been the case. Brennan and I were the only ones here. Even Gaia hadn't been able to follow us.

I sighed a quick breath of relief. I had brought us to the first place that had popped into my mind and I honestly had no idea why I had even thought of Adventureland. But it was for the best. If there was no logical reason, then Mormo wouldn't think to come here.

"Em?" Brennan appealed to me, more firmly this time. "What is going on?"

"I told you that there was more to life than you knew," I reminded him.

"Yes," he acknowledged. "But you hadn't got to the part yet that covered people appearing from thin air and me getting teleported."

"I'm sorry," I sighed. "This is a lot for you to absorb. I know that. And this changes everything. He saw you with me. And that's not good."

I trailed off as my mind raced a mile a minute. Mormo had seen Brennan with me, which put him in danger. My father wouldn't hesitate to hurt him or even kill him to try and get information from him.

"Who was that man?" Brennan questioned calmly.

I glanced at his face and saw that he was back to being unflappable. Any logical person would be freaking out right about now. The fact that Brennan was staying cool and collected was interesting. He must be tapping in to his demi-god abilities and he didn't even realize it.

"My father," I murmured. Brennan was clearly surprised.

"So, Demis don't get along with their parents?"

"No, that's not true. My father is evil. Yours is not. I'm sure you'll get along just fine with Apollo."

He didn't look convinced, but continued. "What about your mother? Can't she help you? Didn't you say that she's the goddess of witchcraft?"

I nodded. "Yes. She's a very powerful witch. But she wants me to go someplace that I don't want to go. She trusts people that I don't and I'm too nervous to seek her out- not just yet."

Brennan stared at me yet again, clearly trying to wrap his mind around everything that I was telling him. I was surprised he was still here at all and not running in the opposite direction as fast as his muscular legs would take him.

"So you don't trust your mother?" he asked, curious.

"I trust her with my life," I answered firmly. "But I don't trust the same people that she does."

"And who does she trust that you don't?" Brennan inquired hesitantly.

"Hades." I chanced a look at his face and found him to be as astonished as I figured he would be.

"As in... the god of the Underworld?" he asked incredulously.

"The one and the same."

"So, everything that you've told me is real. We're part of mythology. Only mythology isn't myth at all. It's reality." Each word he said was carefully enunciated and slowly spoken. I nodded silently.

"And you personally know the god of the Underworld. And I would assume that you know magic as well, since you are the daughter of a witch."

"A very powerful witch, yes." I nodded again. "And yes, I know some magic."

"Is there anything else that I should know?" he asked, his face betraying his nervousness. I hesitated, then nodded.

"There are all kinds of things that you should know. But we don't have time to get into everything right now. The most important thing you should know is that my father is dangerous. He wants to kill me. And since he's seen you with me and I'm certain that he recognized who you really are, you are in danger now, too."

Brennan nodded. "I figured out that part for myself." He turned to me, his handsome face showing not fear, but concern.

"How long have you been running from him?"

I felt my shoulders drop dejectedly. I couldn't help it. "Long enough."

He opened his arms and pulled me into them, holding me close. Breathing into my hair, he said, "You don't have to be afraid anymore. I'm here now. And I'll help you however I can."

I closed my eyes and was surprised to find hot tears welling behind my lids. It had been so long since I had succumbed to weakness or vulnerability of any sort. But so help me... letting him hold me felt so incredibly good right now.

"You can't help me," I whispered. "No one can."

"But I can try," he said grittily. "And I'm very determined." I felt him smile into my hair and I couldn't help but smile, too. He had no idea what he had just gotten into, but there was no help for it now.

"We need to decide where to go," I finally said, reluctantly pulling away from him. "He must have found my house so we can't go back there. Now that he's seen you, he's probably hunting down your house at this very moment. We can't go there, either. Do you live with your father?"

He shook his head. "No. I live in an apartment in town- near the college."

"Well, that's something good at least. We won't have to worry about your dad. And we won't have to explain your upcoming absence."

"My absence?" he raised an eyebrow.

I swallowed. "You're going to have to stay away from your family for a bit. You don't want to lead Mormo to them."

He nodded. "Good thinking. Where should we go?"

I studied his face for a second. He was handsome, calm and perfectly willing to believe everything I had just told him as fact. His hazel eyes returned my stare without flinching and I found that I could get lost in his eyes. They were truly beautiful. I shook those useless thoughts from my head. Thinking like that wasn't going to help us right now.

"You know," I pondered, looking around us once again. "We could just stay right here for the time being. It's remote, there is no one here right now and there's quite a few buildings we could stay in."

He looked at me like I was crazy. "Here? We won't have beds, a kitchen... did I mention beds?"

"Were you expecting a Four Seasons?" I snapped grumpily. "I can conjure just about anything you can think of, including a pillow-top king size bed, if that's what you want. If you're into retro things, I can get you a waterbed. If you want cutting edge, I can get you one of those foam mattress things that don't bounce. Whatever you want, I can do. You won't be exactly roughing it."

"Seriously?" He looked impressed. "You can create an entire king size bed out of thin air?"

I felt exasperated, but reined it in. There's no way that he could possibly know what I was capable of. Sighing, I studied the line of buildings to our left. There was a row of empty restaurants, a house of mirrors, a medical check point and a haunted house. I zeroed back in on the haunted house. Perfect.

"Come with me," I murmured, walking straight toward it.

Brennan stayed by my elbow as we approached the spooky gray-sided home with the faux rickety steps. I knew from experience that the stairs were designed to creak as you climbed them. During the season, bats and cobwebs hung from the porch, but it was bare now and completely clean.

"Here?" Brennan asked incredulously. "You want to sleep in the haunted house? Aren't you afraid of nightmares?"

I looked at him dubiously. "Seriously? I've seen things in real life that would make your head spin. There's nothing in this house that could possibly scare me unless my father is standing on the other side of the door."

I pointed at the black painted door and it flew open, banging into the wall behind it.

"And he's not," I observed. "So, we're good."

To his credit, once again, Brennan didn't even flinch at the use of my other-worldly abilities. Instead, he grinned.

"I'm going to enjoy getting to know you," he announced. "This is going to be fun."

"Fun?" I questioned. "Do you enjoy getting chased by a psychotic madman?"

He shook his head. "Nope. But I enjoy camping out with beautiful women."

He beamed a huge smile at me and I couldn't help but feel warmed from the inside out. He thought I was beautiful. And why did that make me so happy? Most men found me beautiful. Why did Brennan's opinion matter so much?

I sighed. Because he was probably my soul mate. I had a feeling that I was going to get tired of using that as an excuse for everything, even if it did turn out to be true.

We stepped inside and except for the light shining in through the two front windows, it was completely dark.

We were in a large foyer, but it was hard to see anything else. The darkness was shadowy. I snapped my fingers and the lights came on.

"Impressive," Brennan acknowledged. "But maybe we should have left it dark. The ambience in here is sort of spooky-chic, don't you think?"

He was right. The empty, quiet amusement park attraction was creepy, to say the least. And not creepy because of the decorations, but creepy because of the stillness, the emptiness. It was meant to be filled with screaming patrons.

The track that the little train cars traveled on was quiet, the cars apparently stored in another room. I carefully stepped over one metal rail and walked quickly along the track. There had to be a bedroom of sorts in this place.

Brennan followed behind me and I felt his presence with every breath that he took. It was as if we had an invisible tie that bound him to me or vice versa. It pulled us towards each other and it was difficult to resist.

At the end of a darkened hallway, the track passed through a grotesque bedroom taken straight from an old horror movie. A mannequin hung from a noose, dangling in the middle of the room. Red blood-like paint was splattered all over her. Her lifeless eyes seemed to watch us as I examined the rest of our surroundings.

A dusty bed was pushed against the back wall, covered in plastic black spiders. Perfect. Nothing said a good night's rest like arachnids, fake or otherwise. Another dead 'body' was lying on the floor next to the bed in a pool of dried red paint. Apparently, this room was meant to portray a murder scene.

"Charming," Brennan muttered.

"My thoughts exactly," I answered. "Let's clean this place up a bit, shall we?"

I pictured how I wanted the room to be, with a fluffy clean bed, roaring fireplace, picnic basket full of food and lush carpet. Immediately, it was so. I kicked off my shoes and wiggled my toes in the soft rug beneath my feet.

Brennan stared at me in astonishment.

"You're kind of handy to have around, you know that?" He tried to act cool and nonchalant, but I could see the truth in his eyes. He was shaken. And just a little bit terrified. As if to distract himself, he strolled over to the picnic basket and rifled through it, popping a ripe strawberry into his mouth.

Wanting to prove a point, I blurred into motion and pinned him against the wall. With my mouth hovering a scant inch over his, I spoke very softly, very succinctly.

"I don't want you to mistake something," I murmured against his lips. "I'm very dangerous. Don't forget that. It is something that I can't help. I am very, very drawn to you. Perhaps we are soul mates, perhaps we aren't. I guess time will tell. But in the meantime, we need to tread carefully. I don't want you to get hurt."

His chest was hard beneath my fingers, the muscles tight and sinewy. He gazed down at me, his hazel eyes golden in the light.

"I don't think you want to hurt me," he observed. "So I'm not all that afraid. And besides, I'm a demi, too, remember?"

I almost snorted as I backed up just a bit. "You're a demi who didn't even know that he was a demi until today. You have no idea how to tap into your abilities or your strengths. You're the same as a mortal at this point."

His gaze flickered. "But I *am* mortal. Right?"

I nodded. "Yes, you are."

Confusion flitted across his features. "And you're not?"

"No. I'm not. Because both of my parents are immortal, I am immortal too. You would have to appeal to Zeus for immortality." I gulped, because the sudden thought of being separated from Brennan for eternity caused my chest to constrict.

I felt his breathing quicken beneath my fingertips.

"I don't want to be away from you," he admitted, mirroring my own thoughts. It brought a lump to my throat that I couldn't swallow. "Not for a day and definitely not forever. How would I go about appealing to Zeus?"

"You'd have to travel to Mount Olympus in the Spiritlands," I told him. "But we don't have time right this moment. For now, we should probably concentrate on acquainting you with your skills."

He looked at me with interest. "I'm ready any time you are."

"I practice magic on a full stomach the best," I quipped. "Let's eat first."

He shrugged and grabbed my hand, pulling me back to the picnic basket.

"I can't help but notice that there's only one bed," he said slyly, grinning as he eyed it.

"Because only one will fit in this room," I explained. "Don't get any ideas."

"I would never," he replied a little over-zealously and I laughed.

"Never?" I raised an eyebrow doubtfully.

He laughed, a throaty, sexy sound that made my heart palpitate.

"Well, maybe I will at some point," he admitted. I had to laugh at his honesty.

"Well, for today," I began, "We're going to work on your skills. You'll be too tired for any of your 'ideas'."

"We'll see about that," he replied cockily, swaggering back to the picnic basket to grab another strawberry.

I smirked. Within an hour, he'd be begging for mercy.

# Chapter Seven

"So, how much longer do you want to do this?" Brennan asked calmly.

He wasn't even a little bit out of breath. I was drenched in sweat from my mental exertions and I could quite literally kill for an ice cold drink. But I didn't want him to know that.

I leveled my gaze at him. He stood with his arms crossed across the room, his tanned brow furrowed.

"Are you tired?" I asked innocently.

"No," he answered. "But I'm hungry."

"I need for you to master this," I insisted, gritting my teeth. "As you saw today, traveling god-style is the best way to go. It's saved my butt a hundred times."

He shrugged. "It doesn't appear that I can do it."

"That's because you're still thinking like a mortal," I mused. "You've got to open your mind and start thinking like a god. You're the son of Apollo, after all. Maybe we should focus on other abilities and come back to this one. Have you noticed that you're able to do something special? Something that normal people can't do?"

"There are a few things," he admitted. "But I've always tried to put them out of my mind- tried to pretend that they didn't happen."

"Like?" I prompted.

"Oh, you know..." he drawled. "The normal stuff. I can heal faster than the average person. I don't get hurt as often. Sometimes, I can see something that is about to happen. It plays in my head like a movie and then it actually occurs."

"So, you can see the future and you heal at a supernatural rate," I repeated. "Is that it? Because I thought it was going to be something impressive."

He grinned and I sucked my breath in. By the gods, he was handsome. I would chalk that up to another gift inherited from his father. I just wouldn't point it out to him.

"Is there anything else?" I asked, somewhat nervously.

"Perhaps," he said slowly. He finally seemed a little nervous. "Sometimes, very rarely, I can make things happen. I don't know how, but I think about something and it just... happens. Maybe not exactly as I imagined it, but it still happens to some degree."

"Interesting," I breathed. He could not only see the future, but he could make it happen, too. That could certainly come in handy.

"Maybe," he acknowledged. "But the problem is, I apparently haven't mastered it. It doesn't usually work."

"And you never wondered about these things?" I demanded. "You never once wondered why you were different? Why you could do things that your friends couldn't?"

He scowled. "Of course I have. But what answers could I possibly come to on my own? Being the son of a god isn't exactly a logical conclusion."

"I suppose not," I answered tiredly. "There are several things that it looks like we should work on. I really wish that we could get my mother's help. She's very good in situations like this."

"Then why don't we?" he suggested. I tried to ignore the way his black shirt was clinging to his muscular chest. "Why can't we?"

"I've already explained this," I replied grumpily. "I can't let her find us. She wants to take me to Hades to have the curse removed. I can't let her do that. I just don't trust him. My life is rather important to me. I don't trust Hades with it."

"So, let's go to your mother, then," he offered. "We can travel to… wherever it is that she lives. And the second she acts as though she's going to try something, you can whisk us out of there with just a little wriggle of your nose."

"I'm not on *Bewitched*," I sighed. "And I'm not sure that I would be strong enough to get us out of there if my mother tried to prevent it. She's *very* powerful."

"And you love and trust her," he pointed out gently. "I think that she would respect your wishes enough to comply with them. Really. I mean, clearly she loves you. She's been searching for you. Can't you trust her enough to try?"

He knew exactly which buttons to push and I cringed. It was true. My mother loved me more than anything in the world. And Brennan's idea was almost a good one. If we appeared to her in her home in the Spiritlands, perhaps we could appeal to her to just help us and let us leave.

"Maybe," I answered cautiously. "I wonder...would it be better to surprise her or gain her cooperation first?"

"And how would you go about doing that?" he answered curiously. "Don't tell me that she has a cell phone."

I rolled my eyes. "No. The goddess of witchcraft does not have a cell phone," I answered wryly. "But she visits me in my dreams. If she comes to me tonight, I'll bring it up."

"Interesting," he replied quietly. "You can visit other people's dreams? Then you would find mine fascinating lately. You've been in all of them."

My heart beat faster. "You wouldn't continue with the same dreams once I was there," I explained. "I would just fill up your mind and we would have a conversation, just as if I was there in person."

"But you *are* here in person," he murmured, crossing the room in four long strides to stand in front of me. "You're right in front of me."

"Yes," I murmured, running my hands upward on his chest. Sliding my fingers along his neck, I leaned in to kiss him, but the startling desire to suck out his soul caused me to drop my hand and quickly step away.

"What is it?" he asked, his eyes narrowed. "What's wrong? Why do you always do that?"

"There are more things that you don't know," I answered weakly. "Things about me. And I don't know that I want to explain them right now."

"Now is the very best time," he answered firmly. "I think I have a right to know."

He took a step toward me, but I gestured him back. He stilled in his tracks.

"Maybe," I acknowledged. "But that doesn't mean that I want to get into it right now."

"Please?" he added, his handsome face uncertain. Somehow, that boyish quality did me in. Despite myself, I felt my heart soften. "Tell me about you," he continued. "Everything."

I sighed. He was right. If he was going to be close to me, he deserved to know.

"My full name is Empusa," I began softly. "You already know who my parents are. I was born immortal. You know that I am cursed because my father traded my soul for his own freedom from the Underworld. What you don't know, is what that curse entails."

I glanced at his face. He was watching me intently, standing motionlessly just two feet away. I could reach out and touch him—I ached to do it- but I clenched my fists instead. I had to get through this.

"Go on," he urged quietly. "Tell me."

I nodded. "In order to stay immortal and young, I have to steal mortal souls. I have to breathe them in. In order to stay alive in between, I have to drink mortal blood."

He froze, absolutely still, his eyes widened. "You're a vampire?"

I shook my head quickly. "No. Of course not. The vampyre are legends, not real. They were created to make sense out of nightmarish events that mortal minds couldn't process otherwise."

"You mean, like your father drinking their blood?" Brennan raised an eyebrow. "I assume that your father was like this before he transferred the curse to you?"

I nodded miserably. "It's possible that my father was the true source of vampire legend," I conceded.

He moved to me, pulling me to him. He placed his hand on my chest. "Your heart beats," he observed quietly. "So, you're not a vampire."

"I told you that," I replied. He nodded.

"Your skin is warm," he pointed out, as he slid his fingers along my arm.

I nodded silently, not trusting my voice. I hadn't realized how nerve-wracking it would be to expose myself to Brennan. I trusted him and he could stomp on that trust if he wanted. I had never felt so vulnerable.

"Are you tempted to steal my soul every time that I'm near you?" he asked quietly.

Lifting a hand, he brushed it across my cheek. I wanted to melt into his arms, but I restrained myself.

"They say that it causes vampires physical pain to be near humans and not drink their blood," he said as he watched my face. "Do I cause you pain, Empusa?"

He sounded concerned for me- for my well-being- far more than he seemed to be about his own. My heart warmed even more. Except for my mother, I had never known someone who thought about me before they thought about themselves. It was... huge.

"No, you do not cause me pain," I told him. "I'm not a vampire. But it takes a lot of restraint to not hurt you sometimes. Every once in awhile, I feel an overwhelming need to take your soul from you."

"What about my blood?" he asked curiously. "Do you want to drink my blood? Is it hard to resist?"

I shook my head. "No. I don't really get cravings for blood. I simply know when I need to eat- I get tired, pale. And when that happens, I must find someone to drink from."

"I doubt you have trouble finding willing donors," he said wryly. And then his brow wrinkled. "You don't... kill people, do you?"

For the first time, he sounded nervous- like he wasn't sure that he wanted to hear my answer. And I didn't want to answer him.

"I don't kill them by drinking their blood," I confirmed, leaving out a key piece of information. I killed them by taking their souls. And Brennan was astute. He took one look at my face and knew I was holding something back.

"What are you hiding?" he asked gently. "You're not telling me something."

I swallowed hard and then swallowed again.

"I'm very dangerous," I reminded him. "I don't want you to lower your guard around me."

"If you aren't tempted to drink my blood, then what threat are you to me?"

"Your soul is more valuable to you than your blood could ever be," I explained abruptly. "Your body creates more blood to replace any that is lost. You have one soul. If it is lost or taken from you, then you will die."

"So, when you steal someone's soul from them…" his voice trailed off as cold realization dawned on him. "You *do* kill people."

"But I don't like it," I rushed to say. "I hate it, actually. And I have faith that once everything is sorted out and my father is once again in the Underworld where he belongs, that all of the souls that I have taken will be returned to the Underworld where they can live in peace for eternity."

"How do you choose?" he asked slowly. "How do you decide who will die?"

I hadn't noticed until now that he had stepped backwards- away from me. The distance felt like a stake in my heart. I gulped. I hated that he had made such a difference in me already. I hated that I cared what he thought.

"I choose people who are about to die anyway," I murmured. The words welled up painfully on my tongue and I hated to say them. "That way, it doesn't feel like I am actually ending their lives."

He stared at me, his hazel eyes pensive. "Like my uncle," he stated calmly.

I gulped. I had never, in over a thousand years, had been forced to stand in front of a family member and held accountable for killing someone. It was a hideous feeling. The accusation in Brennan's eyes impaled me and I felt like I couldn't breathe.

I nodded once, the only movement I was able to make.

From here, I could hear his heartbeat race, louder and harder than it had beat a moment ago. He was frightened. Or upset. Or angry. Maybe all three of those things. And he was silent.

I waited for an uncomfortable moment.

Then another.

Finally I couldn't stand it.

"Say something," I pleaded.

"What would you like for me to say?" he asked. "You killed my uncle. I don't know how I'm supposed to process that. I feel like a traitor because I'm still so drawn to you with this overwhelming attraction. I don't know how I'm supposed to feel."

His voice was tight, his hands clenched at his sides. I had never felt so helpless.

"I'm so sorry," I whispered. "I never asked to be… what I am. I pray every night that I will be given my old life back, that my father will be captured and returned to the Underworld."

He nodded curtly. "That's part of what makes this so hard. You're a victim, too."

He turned away from me and walked to the fireplace, holding his hands out to the warmth. The flames reflected from his eyes, making them seem golden and I flew to his side, grasping his arm.

"Brennan," I began softly. "Please believe me. I really liked your uncle. He was ready to go. I didn't hurt him. He didn't feel a thing. And someday, he will be with his daughter, where he belongs."

Brennan gazed down at me. "And until then? Until then, where is his soul?"

I averted my gaze. "I don't know," I admitted. "I have no idea. I think it's in limbo."

He looked away, staring once more into the flames. "Empusa, I'm still angry with you for choosing my uncle. But I'm also furious with your father for doing this to you in the first place."

"But you understand, don't you, that I had to?" I beseeched him. "I didn't want to."

"I understand that, yes," he nodded. "And I also understand that you can turn it around. All you have to do is stand in front of Hades and he will un-do the curse- which will free you from its grasp and will release all of the souls you've taken. I don't understand why you haven't done so already."

When he said it in such a way, it did make me seem like a monster. I was letting my own fears, my own need for survival, interfere with doing what was right for all of the souls that I had taken over the years. It wasn't that I hadn't worried about them- it was just that I blocked it out so that the worry didn't consume me. But it was here now, front and center, and I had to face it.

"I understand what you're saying," I acknowledged. "But it's harder than it sounds. If I make a wrong move, perhaps all of those souls will be lost. I couldn't bear that, either."

"Inaction doesn't accomplish anything, though," he said solemnly. And I knew he was right.

"I know," I admitted. "I know. I promise you. I'll seek my mother tonight in her dreams. I won't wait for her to come to me. I'll go to her instead. I'll try to sort this out and do the right thing. If I do that, can you forgive me?"

He looked at me, his expression both tender and hesitant. "I already forgave you," he said quietly. "But I can't help being angry with you. I'll work through it."

My heart dropped into my toes. The idea that he was upset with me chilled me to the bone- even as I knew that he couldn't help what he felt. But he was being so strong about everything that I felt more drawn to him than ever.

"You're really amazing," I whispered. "Thank you."

"Don't mention it," he said curtly. "Seriously- let's stop talking about it. Let's just get some rest and hopefully you can talk to you mother."

He turned his back and began pulling the covers down on the bed. "You can have the bed," he said quietly. "I'll take the floor."

"That's ridiculous," I answered. "We can share the bed. I'm not going to attack you in your sleep."

"I wasn't worried about that," he replied, turning back to me. "We have this attraction between us. And I'm pretty sure we shouldn't act on it right now. Sleeping together might not be the best idea."

"Oh, for Heaven's sake," I muttered, brushing past him to drop onto the bed and take my shoes off. "We're adults. We can restrain ourselves, right?"

He didn't answer.

Glancing up at him, I raised an eyebrow. "Right?"

"I suppose," he replied, although he didn't appear convinced. He sighed. "Honestly, I can hardly keep my hands off of you right now and we're not even in bed yet. What have you done to me?"

I opened my mouth, but before I could speak, Brennan did.

"Let me guess. It's part of your curse?"

I nodded. "I have characteristics of a Siren. People are drawn to me. You would think it would be a blessing, but it's not. I can't become close to anyone because I might kill them. I've been very alone for a long time."

He stared at me for a long moment. I could practically hear the seconds ticking away before he finally sighed raggedly and opened his arms.

"Come here," he commanded softly.

I didn't even realize that my feet were moving before I found myself in his embrace. Burying my head against his chest, I inhaled his scent and closed my eyes. If I could, I would stay right here forever. But I couldn't and I knew that.

Pulling away, I looked up at him and was surprised to find that my eyelashes were wet.

"I know that we haven't known each other for every long, but I honestly feel like I've known you forever- like I've always been waiting for you. I promise you right now that I will do whatever I can to fix this. If you can just be patient…" My voice caught in my throat.

He nodded and lowered his lips to mine.

"I'm not going anywhere."

# Chapter Eight

It was very hard to fall asleep when the son of Apollo was sharing your bed, that much was certain. Because Brennan was gigantic, he took up the majority of our sleeping space. On top of that, his muscled arms and legs were pressed against me, causing me to grit my teeth with pent-up frustration.

Every cell in my body longed to reach out for him, to draw him near. But he was right. We shouldn't act on that attraction yet... not at this juncture. There were so many things unanswered and convoluted. I sighed and flipped over onto my other side, which of course didn't make anything better. It only served to press his muscles against my back rather than my side. He was also very, very warm. I wondered if it had anything to do with his father being the god of the sun.

I could tell from his even, slow breathing that he was asleep already, so I tossed a few silent names his way. It was so unfair that men could sleep at anytime, anywhere. I jammed a pillow over my head to block out all semblance of light. If I wasn't able to sleep, then I couldn't speak with my mother.

In order to enter someone's dreams, you had to be asleep yourself. You had to enter sleep with a purpose of transporting yourself into their dream the second that you drifted into sleep. It was an art. And it was an art that was impossible if you weren't able to sleep in the first place.

I groaned.

"Just relax." Brennan's deep voice resonated through the quiet room. "You're never going to fall asleep if you get frustrated."

"I thought you were sleeping," I answered tiredly, rolling back to my other side to look at him.

His eyes were open and he was staring at me, his topaz gaze liquid in the night. He appraised me quietly and even though he didn't touch me, his stare brushed over my skin as potently as his fingers ever could. The tension between us was palpable, I could practically breathe it in and taste it.

"I was," he replied huskily. "And now I'm not. You're restless."

"I'm sorry," I apologized. "I really don't mean to keep you up. You need your rest too."

He opened his arms. "Come here," he instructed. I stared at him hesitantly.

"I'm not sure that's a great idea," I admitted, still eyeing him. He had taken his shirt off and the muscles rippled across his broad chest as he moved. He was Apollo's son through and through.

He smiled and I felt warmed from head to toe. "I promise I'll behave," he said solemnly. I paused a scant second longer before I folded into his arms, leaning my forehead against the warm skin of his chest.

He smelled like heaven and his warmth enveloped me like a blanket. I sighed contentedly.

"Okay. Now relax," he instructed me again. "Nothing will disturb you. I promise you that."

He sounded so sure of himself, so brave. He had absolutely no idea of what kind of monsters actually existed out in the world. His mortal mind had never seen true evil. But I had. And I knew that in his current, untrained state, Brennan was no match for any of it. But regardless, I did feel comforted and safe in his strong arms. I would worry about training him tomorrow. Tonight, I would let him hold me.

My eyelids closed and I felt his lips softly graze my temple.

"Sleep well," he said gently. I snuggled closer to him, absorbing his radiant warmth. Picturing my mother in my mind, I ran her through my consciousness on a loop. Before I knew it, I was drifting off and I found myself standing in a cold, hazy place.

I looked around in confusion.

This wasn't my mother's dream. It looked like eternal stark winter here. White fog swirled in cold funnels, while gray sky closed in all around me. Dead, blackened trees dotted the horizon and the wind howled. I shivered, rubbing my arms to warm them. My body heat was being sucked out more and more by the second.

This had to be the Wastelands. I'd heard of it before. It was a place that existed between reality and the subconscious. The Fates, the three sisters who used to control destiny, had used this place as a punishment for those who dared go against them. The Fates took their emotions and their souls...and left them here.

I looked around at the vast expanse surrounding me. That didn't explain why I was here now. The Fates had been imprisoned in the Underworld. They couldn't do a thing to anyone.

As I pondered it, I couldn't help but notice the horrifyingly sad atmosphere. Every moment that I was here, I felt more and more forlorn and sad. It was quickly becoming overwhelming. I closed my eyes, anxious to leave. If a person spent much time here, they would rapidly grow suicidal.

"Wait," a deep voice said. "Don't leave yet."

My eyes flew open to find a man standing in front of me, almost consumed by the swirling fog. His long black robes seemed to swirl with the mist, all the way down to his bare toes. His head was shaved and inky black Egyptian script was tattooed on his hands. His eyes were onyx black and glittered as he stared at me. It was impossible to guess his age. But if I had to hazard one, I would say he was ancient.

"Yes?" I answered, as bravely as I could. I forced my feet to remain still and not step away.

"I was sent here by your mother," the man said. "I brought you to this neutral place because it is safer."

"My mother?" I asked. "Where is she?"

He ignored my question. "Hecate knows that you seek her," he said quietly, his voice hoarse with years and wisdom. "It is not safe for you to find her just now. You must stay away."

My eyes narrowed on their own accord. "How do I know that you aren't lying? Perhaps you have done something with her yourself."

The man threw his head back and laughed, a creepy, unsettling sound, and in that instant, I realized that I knew him.

"I've seen you before," I whispered. "Somewhere. But I cannot remember where. Do I know you?"

He shook his head. "No, you don't. But I know you."

As he moved, I caught a whiff of his scent and recognition dawned on me. "You were with Harmonia in the Underworld," I said cautiously. "Your name is Ahmose, correct?"

He nodded. "Yes, that is my name. And yes, I've been with Harmonia in many places throughout the years. But I am here now, to help you. Your mother and Harmonia both wished it so."

Harmonia was the goddess of peace and contentment. In the not so distant past, she had battled the Fates in order to secure the freedom of the Olympians. During the struggles, the Fates had sent Harmonia's daughter, Raquel, to the Underworld. I had accidentally come across her and had taken care of her until Harmonia could find us. I knew that she would be forever grateful to me because of that. If her right-hand man was here now, it was because Harmonia wished to help me. Knowing this, I chose to believe Ahmose and nodded.

"Fine. My mother sent you. Is she alright?"

He studied me, his black eyes gleaming. "Your mother is the most powerful witch in the world. She is fine. But it is not safe for you to seek her currently, yet it is not safe for you to linger in the mortal world unprotected, either."

"I'm not going to Hades," I cried determinedly. "Can't you see that we cannot trust him?"

Ahmose held up a calm hand. "Hush now, young one. I was not speaking of going to Hades or even Zeus. Before your curse is lifted, much will come to pass. You must seek out the third brother, Poseidon. You draw strength from water- so what better place for you to seek refuge than an underwater world? Your mother wishes it so and Poseidon is expecting you. You must trade your bracelet for safe refuge in Poseidon's world. Your mother has arranged it."

Confusion swirled around me.

"My mother no longer wishes for me to return to the Underworld? Why not? What has happened? What changed her mind? And my bracelet? I cannot! It is enchanted to save my life. She would never ask me to give it away."

Ahmose shook his head. "There is no time to discuss it. You must leave here. It is only safe to linger here for a few minutes. The despair will overwhelm you otherwise. Your mother had to barter your bracelet- it is a sign to Poseidon that you trust him, a sign of respect. You must give it to him in exchange for safe refuge. I imagine that he will return it to you when you leave his world. Leave here now, Empusa- but don't remain too long in the mortal world before you go to Poseidon. Your safety depends upon it."

He waved his hand and I was suddenly waking up, still curled in the safety of Brennan's strong arms.

My brow was damp from anxious sweat and I impatiently pushed my hair out of my eyes. That was a strange and intriguing experience at the same time. Why had my mother sent a message through Ahmose rather than just coming herself? Something was going on- and I was sure that I wouldn't like it if I knew what it was.

I glanced at my watch. The luminous hands said that it was just after 3:00 am. Dreamwalking always took up more time than it seemed. Brennan breathed deeply and evenly, his arms still wrapped securely around me even in sleep. I smiled and brushed his hair back with my fingers. He was boyish as he slept and I couldn't help but stare at him.

His cheekbones were chiseled, his lashes long. He had a very Roman nose, proud and aqualine. It gave just the right amount of character to his face. His lips were soft and pink and I ached to bend and kiss them.

"So, do it then."

I startled as he read my mind, then laughed. "You faker. I thought you were sleeping."

He tightened his embrace around me before he answered. "I was. But I'm a very light sleeper. When you woke up, you woke me up. If you want to kiss me, just do it."

I pulled away from him so that I was able to freely move. Running my hand along his cheek, I bent my head and kissed him lightly on the mouth. He tasted like youth and sunshine. I couldn't help but moan into the kiss and he grabbed me again, flattening me against his chest.

"I think I've been waiting for you," I murmured, stroking his collar bone.

"Really?" He eyed me. "For how long?"

"Forever," I answered quietly. "You were made for me. I know it."

His breathing quickened and I could hear his heart race. Cautiously, I moved backward a little bit. We couldn't get carried away.

"No," he growled, pulling me back to him. "I never want to be away from you again. I've only been alive for eighteen years, but when I am with you, I feel ageless... and I start regretting all of the years that you've lived without me. I'm jealous of time itself, because it was with you when I wasn't."

"Silly mortal," I laughed. "You're jealous of time? Don't be. Time is nothing. We can bend it to our will, laugh at it, stomp on it. You'll see- once this is over and we ask Zeus for your immortality… you'll see. Time will fall away."

"What will happen," Brennan began, "If something happens to me before that? Will I die like a mortal?"

It felt like my stomach was wrapped in a vise grip at his words and I gasped. "Don't even say that. Nothing will happen to you. I won't allow it. And besides, demi's are harder to injure or kill than a mortal. It would take a lot to hurt you."

He nodded. "I'm not worried, simply curious. And slightly uncomfortable having my girlfriend protect my life. I need to learn some skills before my manhood gets sucked away."

I laughed again. "I don't think you have anything to worry about, you've got plenty of 'manhood.' But you're right. You need skills. We'll work on them again in the morning. Well, later in the morning."

He chuckled and we snuggled even more closely together. I closed my eyes once again. It didn't matter what we had to face in order to get this curse reversed or to get Zeus to grant Brennan immortality. I would do anything.

\* \* \*

We stood on the top arch of the Gryphon roller coaster hundreds of feet above the ground. We were so high up that the birds sitting below us on the fairway looked like tiny specks. The wind whipped wildly around us and we constantly had to re-balance ourselves on the steel track so that we didn't fall.

"Why again, are we up here?" Brennan shouted to me as he balanced precariously on the edge. He almost slipped, then righted himself.

"Because you need an incentive. You need to move us from here to the ground so that we don't fall to our deaths."

"You won't die," he growled.

"True," I answered cheerfully. "So move us to the ground before *you* fall to your death."

He glared at me for a moment, before his brow furrowed in concentration. Far below us, dead leaves rattled as they blew along the ground. Another wind gust buckled my knees and I swayed to combat it, reaching out to hold onto Brennan. There was no way in hell that I would let him fall, but I wasn't going to announce that. He needed this.

Brennan's brow remained furrowed for a few minutes longer, then he scowled. "It's not happening. I'm never going to be able to do it!"

He opened his eyes as we teetered on the thick orange rolled bars of the coaster's track. I wasn't scared of heights, but being up here in the wind without anything to hold onto but each other was even making me feel queasy.

"Just put us on the ground," he urged. "I can practice down there just as easily."

"No, you can't," I answered calmly, swerving into him as the wind blew sharply once more. I readjusted my footing and glancing away from him, I stared at the lake. We could see for miles across it from here, as well as every inch of the amusement park. It seemed so eerie when no one was here.

"Focus. Picture exactly where you want us to be, focus on every minute detail of it. Picture your limbs fading from here…and it will happen."

His forehead scrunched again as the wind blew his hair away from his face. Long minutes passed and sweat formed on his brow from his heavy concentration.

"You can do it," I urged quietly, clutching his forearm tightly in the wind.

He opened his eyes. "I can't. I'm sorry."

I sighed and reached for him. But as I did, I lost my footing. I barely had time to scream before I was suddenly on the ground, scooped into Brennan's arms.

"What the…" my voice trailed off as I gazed up at him.

"I guess you did give me the incentive," he mused.

"I didn't do that on purpose," I insisted, tightening my grasp around his neck.

"Whatever you say," he grinned.

"I didn't. But what a nice result. You saved me from falling and you moved us! Do it again! Put me down and transport yourself somewhere."

Obligingly, he set me gently down and scrunched his eyes closed. A muscle in his cheek ticked with concentration and within a minute, he was gone. Whirling around, I found him standing on the roof of a nearby maintenance building, grinning like crazy.

I clapped in appreciation and he bowed. Before I could blink, he was standing next to me once again.

"Show off," I laughed.

"You were right," he admitted. "It was easy once I broke through my own mental block. I feel like I could do anything right now."

"You practically can," I pointed out. "You don't even know the half of it yet. And I can't wait to show you."

"So show me," he commanded, reaching out to pull me to him. I backed out of his reach.

"I can't just now," I told him, watching in amusement as he glared at me. "We have someplace that we need to go first. I can show you the other things as we go along."

"Where are we going?" he asked curiously. Once again, he didn't seem nervous in the slightest. He trusted me and that knowledge warmed me from the core of my heart to the tips of my toes.

"Oh, we're going someplace interesting," I answered, as vaguely as I could.

He raised an eyebrow. "Such as? What's the zip code?"

"Where we're going doesn't have a zip code," I answered with a smile. "Can you swim?"

He narrowed his eyes. "Of course. Why?"

"Because we're going to pay a visit to Poseidon."

# Chapter Nine

We stood with our toes hanging over the white fiberglass hull of a boat that I had conjured from thin air. The blue sparkling waters of the Aegean Sea rocked us gently and Brennan turned to me.

"You can't be serious?"

We were so far out to sea that even the sea gulls couldn't find us and I smiled.

"Dead serious. We have to jump in and start swimming, then I can transport us to Poseidon's gates. But we have to jump in first. It's just the way it is. Why? Are you scared?"

He scowled. "Of course not. That's ridiculous. Why would I be afraid of jumping into the middle of the ocean without a wetsuit or oxygen tank?" he asked teasingly. "It just seems silly that you can't just deliver us into his city without getting all wet, that's all."

"Are you so sweet that you're going to melt?" I asked saucily. "Because I really don't think that is a concern."

He laughed, wiggling his toes.

"Tell me more about Poseidon before we go. What's he like?"

I pictured Poseidon's solemn, stark face in my mind. "He's… um… stern."

"Stern?" Brennan raised a golden eyebrow. "Stern as in unfriendly?"

"Stern as in… sort of rigid. He's very fair with almost all things except for women. He seems to enjoy… shall we say, taking women by force."

Brennan's mouth dropped open. "Seriously? Poseidon enjoys raping women?"

I shrugged. "Apparently. But I'm not worried about myself. My mother would never send me to him without procuring my safety first."

"You're certain?"

"Of course not. But I know my mother would die to protect me. She would never send me to him without brokering a deal for my complete safety. I know that."

Brennan didn't look thoroughly convinced, so I grasped his arm and squeezed it gently.

"It will be fine, I promise."

He gave me a wry look. "You can't promise me that."

I rolled my eyes. "Quit being such a girl. We'll do what we have to do. Do you want to be together?"

He nodded. "Of course I do. And I'm not being a girl. I'm just worried about you. I don't want anything to happen to you."

"Then we'll have to trust my mother and just do this. We can handle whatever comes. Do you trust that?"

He studied me quietly, his hazel eyes flashing liquid gold against the azure backdrop of the sky. "Yes. And I will go with you anywhere."

"I know," I smiled. Catching him off guard, I gave him a shove and he went flying into the sea. Within a few seconds, he re-emerged from the surface, sputtering.

"I can't believe you just did that!" he shouted, shaking the water from his hair as he tread water.

"Why not?" I laughed. "You already told me that you can swim and that you would go with me anywhere. I thought that was permission."

Before I could blink, he was standing beside me once again, dripping water onto the boat deck in fat droplets.

"And *you* already taught me to teleport," he reminded me laughingly, scooping me into his arms and tossing me. I sprawled into the air and then landed clumsily into the water, sinking into the dark blue depths. From under here, the boat above looked like a massive white whale. I kicked away from it and emerged a few yards away.

"Nice," I commended him. "I'll have to keep in mind that you're a tricky one."

He dove cleanly into the water and I stared nervously around me, waiting for him to appear. He grabbed my legs before I could locate him and pulled me under.

As I slid beneath the surface, his hands glided smoothly along the length of my leg, stopping at my hips. He pulled me to him under water, the length of his body hard and warm. I clung to his neck, staring into his eyes. Here, in the tranquil, underwater abyss, we felt like the only two people in the world. But we weren't. And as my oxygen ran out, reality called.

Kicking to the surface, I pulled him by the hand and we emerged together, bobbing in the blue water.

"As much as I'd like to play all day, we have things to do," I reminded him.

"Spoil sport," he muttered, trying to pull me to him again. I almost relented, just for a minute. The sensation of his strong hands on my wet body was tantalizing, to say the least. But I knew it wasn't smart to get distracted right now. Too much was at stake. If all went well, we would have forever to play.

"Let's go," I urged him, tugging his hand. "Take a deep breath. We're going to swim downward and I'll hopefully get us transported to Poseidon's gates."

"Hopefully?" Brennan repeated doubtfully.

"*Probably*," I revised. "I've never actually been there before. But I think I can do it."

"That's confidence inspiring," Brennan grinned, grasping my hand. "Well, I have faith in you. So, let's do it."

"Ready?"

He nodded and we both took a deep breath and dove beneath the sparkling surface. We swam down, down, down and I concentrated on Poseidon's gates. It was a feat harder than it sounded since I had never actually seen them. But the essence of the thought must have been enough because a scant moment later, we were standing on dry land in front of enormously tall glittering golden gates.

Brennan and I both stared at them for a moment and then each other. We were standing on sand beneath the water, but we were perfectly dry. Not one drop of water was on either of us. It was as though we'd never been in the water at all, as though the sea wasn't all around us.

"What the hell?" Brennan breathed.

"I don't know," I answered. "I've never been here before."

He looked up at the dark blue sea above us. "It's like we're inside a bubble," he observed. "The water is all around us, but it can't close in on us."

I nodded. "I'm guessing that this gate is enchanted. It's probably a portal. Once we enter it, we'll be in an entirely different world."

I could see Brennan swallow, but he didn't voice his hesitation. Instead, he grasped my hand once again. "Well, what are we waiting for?"

"Nothing," I answered, reaching out with a shaky hand to push at the gates. Nothing happened. The cold golden bars remained rigidly closed.

"Hell," I muttered. "How do we get in?"

"Don't look at me," Brennan quipped, his hands splayed open at his sides. "I'm the newbie here."

I rolled my eyes and pondered our situation. There was a keyhole in the large golden door-handle, but I didn't have a key. I sighed, but as I did, I recognized a pounding sound coming from somewhere. Brennan and I both turned to find the source of the noise.

A huge gray stallion thundered toward us from the distance, its black mane and tail streaming into the wind behind it as it tossed its head proudly. Something hung from its mouth and as it drew closer, I saw that it was a key.

"Is that..."Brennan murmured.

"Yes. It's a key," I confirmed.

"Unbelievable," he shook his head.

"Get used to it," I instructed. "Things are different in the world of the gods. You've only just begun."

He shook his head again, but he didn't have time to say anything. The horse had reached us and knelt onto one front knee so that I could take the key from its mouth. Its eyes were large and wild and I was slightly nervous to reach so close to its enormous teeth. But I did and he didn't hurt me.

Inserting the key into the massive lock, I turned it and the doors swung open.

"Welcome to my home."

The words came from behind and I spun to find Poseidon himself standing where the horse had just been. I felt like smacking myself. Of course- one of his symbols was the horse. I should have known it was him. His face was sharp and fierce, his hair a sandy blonde. Like most of the Olympians, he had silver eyes and they glittered now.

I dipped my head in deference.

"Poseidon. Thank you for having us."

Poseidon eyed me up and down, his gaze sliding from my legs, to my breasts and finally to my face.

"Oh, I'd like to have you," he confirmed. "But I promised your mother that I would not. And as you know, she is a formidable woman."

I felt like smirking. I knew my mother had secured my safety. I could feel Brennan's incredulous stare on my back, but I didn't turn around.

"This is Brennan, the son of Apollo," I introduced him to Poseidon. "Brennan, this is Poseidon, the god of the sea."

"It's very nice to meet you," Brennan said politely, mimicking the way that I had dipped my head. Poseidon gave him a cursory glance and a nod before he returned his attention to me.

"We will go to my palace, where we shall dine," he announced. "And then I will hide you away in one of my other properties. Do not fear. Mormo shall not find you. And even if he does, he shall not gain entry. Do you have something for me?"

He held out his hand expectantly and I paused briefly, fear freezing in my heart. I felt as though I shouldn't take my bracelet off, as though I should protect it. But my mother had promised it to him and I had to trust that she knew what she was doing. I slipped it off my wrist and dropped it into his hand. He tucked it into the folds of his cloak.

"You are very beautiful," Poseidon announced matter-of-factly. "Even more so than your mother and in a very different way."

I stared at him. What was one supposed to say to that? "Thank you," I murmured. He nodded.

"Come," he ordered, marching ahead of us in long strides.

Poseidon was wearing a short kilt-type thing made from slats of leather. It was belted at his waist and he wore a metal breast-plate. His muscles bulged and he looked like he had just stepped from a gladiator's coliseum. I watched Brennan gaping at him and couldn't help but smile. It would be amusing to see his reactions from here on out.

We stepped through the gates and it was truly another world. Everything was covered in muted light even though there was no visible source. Beautiful shades of blues and greens abounded, accented by reds, corals, pinks and oranges. It was an absolutely breathtaking underwater paradise. Only, we weren't in water. It boggled the mind.

"Actually," Poseidon called over his shoulder, "I think you will stay the night before I move you. It will please my wife to have visitors."

"He's married?" Brennan whispered to me. Before I could warn him that gods could hear practically anything, Poseidon answered him.

"Of course I am."

Brennan looked at me sheepishly. As time went on, he would be able to hone his own senses and he would realize that he too had the super-sensitive hearing of a god. But we would work on that later.

As we strolled down the bronzed walkways, I couldn't help but stare around us. It was amazing here. An entire underwater civilization surrounded us. People strolled, worked and shopped. Quaint shops and tidy homes made from stone lined the streets and in the distance, a large palace rose from the horizon. It seemed to be built from glass.

I heard Brennan suck in his breath as he saw it and I couldn't help but feel the same sense of awe. The glass walls of the castle glistened majestically, seemingly drawing us nearer.

"Your home is beautiful," I murmured to Poseidon. He nodded.

"Yes, it is. We are very comfortable here."

"You say that you have 'other properties'?" Brennan asked curiously as he examined our surroundings. Poseidon looked annoyed that Brennan had spoken at all, but he still chose to answer.

"Yes, of course I do. I am the god of the sea. All waters fall under my realm, including any small islands that they may contain."

Well, that was vague enough. So, apparently, any island in the world belonged to Poseidon. Good to know. And that meant he was probably going to stash us on a remote island somewhere.

We had made it to the flower-lined walkways that lead to the palace. I gazed ahead of us and it was truly something out of a fairy-tale. The walls were, in fact, made from thick glass. You couldn't see through it to the inside of the palace, but they sparkled like diamonds in the light. It was mesmerizing.

"How is Amphitrite?" I inquired of his wife politely as we climbed the path to the front doors. Large palace guards moved aside to allow our passage and I turned to Poseidon for his answer. He smirked.

"She is as she has always been. But you will soon see for yourselves."

Brennan caught my eye and he gave me a *what the hell?* expression. I smiled. He would soon learn that the complicated world of the gods was complex and frustrating. So many of the gods were pompous and demanding, while others were fairly kind and just. Poseidon was just to his people, I had heard, but he was certainly not a charmer. He was arrogant to the core.

"Welcome to my home," Poseidon said again as he pushed open his front doors.

We stepped inside and found that the inside of his castle was every bit as beautiful as the outside. Polished glass floors gleamed beneath our feet, beautiful tapestries hung on the walls, sparkling chandeliers hung from the tall ceilings. A massive grand staircase opened into the foyer and as I glanced up, I saw Poseidon's wife poised at the halfway point.

She was waiting for us, that much was for sure. She was posed, probably to allow us to see her in her best light and angle. But she wasn't that beautiful. Her hair was mousy brown and hung limply around her shoulders. Her eyes were also mousy brown and overall, she did actually remind me of a mouse. After she was sure that we had seen her, she finished her descent down the stairs and held out her hand to me.

"Empusa!" she cried joyfully, although her tone was just as staged as her pose. I found myself cringing away from her fake niceties, but covered up by quickly grasping her hand and demurely nodding to her.

"Amphitrite!" I greeted her warmly. "It's been far too long!"

She smiled and hugged me, kissing me quickly on each cheek. "You look beautiful, child," she gushed, but her expression was disapproving. She was very, very insecure because Poseidon was very, very unfaithful.

Amphitrite was suspicious of every beautiful woman that she came across....As though every beautiful woman was out to steal her husband. Not hardly- not *this* woman. I'd rather poke my own eyes out with a sharp stick.

"And who do we have here?" she mused, her gaze running over Brennan's lithe form. "Wait- you don't have to tell me. This must be a son of Apollo!" she exclaimed.

"However did you guess?" I asked wryly.

"Why, I've never seen a son resemble a father more than he does!" she gushed. And it was true. As Brennan stood in the muted, ethereal light of the palace, he could be his father's twin. He was radiant.

"I wish I knew my father," Brennan offered. "If I look so much like him, it would be nice to actually meet him."

"Don't worry," I reassured him. "Someday soon you will."

"Well, enjoy that," Poseidon muttered. "I fear you will be greatly let down. Apollo might be handsome, but he is empty-headed and flighty. I hope *you* possess more substance."

Brennan looked almost irate, but I shook my head slightly at him. We could not anger Poseidon. As guests in his home, we needed to get along with him. I could see that Brennan understood my unspoken plea and he acquiesced, saying nothing. I squeezed his hand.

"Would it be possible for us to rest for just a bit before dinner?" I asked politely. "We are weary from the journey here. Traveling to the bottom of the sea is quite a trip."

"Of course, dear," Amphitrite said cordially, as she clapped her hands for a servant. "Please- go rest. Dinner won't be for another hour."

"Son of Apollo," Poseidon said gruffly, "You go ahead. I need to speak with Empusa alone."

Brennan looked to me questioningly and I nodded. "Go ahead, Brennan. I'll be along shortly." A servant clad in white whisked him away and I stood alone with Poseidon and his wife. He raised his eyebrow at Amphitrite.

"I said alone," he reiterated.

She scowled and took her leave. I knew she didn't want to leave Poseidon alone with me, but she had no other choice. Poseidon had spoken and he wasn't someone to trifle with- even if you were his wife, which in my mind, was a dubious honor.

I stared at him expectantly, waiting for him to say something earth shattering, something that he couldn't say in front of anyone else. I itched to move away from him so that he wouldn't be tempted to touch me. I imagined his fingers to be ice cold, just like his stare. But I resisted my urge and remained with my feet planted and my arms crossed over my chest.

Poseidon crossed the room with long strides and poured ice cold nectar of the gods from a silver pitcher into sparkling crystal glasses. He sipped at his as he offered a glass to me.

"I know that nectar doesn't have the same effect on you as it does on me," he acknowledged as he handed it to me, "But it is still delicious, at any rate."

The nectar of the Olympians kept the gods immortal. It flowed in rivers and creeks in the Spiritlands and the gods drank it to stay young. It didn't help me right now. I had to drink souls for that purpose. But he was right, I discovered, as I sipped at the icy goodness. It was truly delicious, like nothing I had ever tasted.

"You seem pale," he observed, drawing one hand across my cheek. I almost flinched, but didn't. I remained still as he caressed my face. I had been wrong. His hands weren't cold. "Perhaps you should stay the night before we travel on."

"I'm fine," I answered, pulling away from him. "If I just rest for a few minutes before dinner, I will be as good as new."

Lie. All of the teleporting and conjuring and such had left me drained. I needed blood to replenish my energy. But I would never tell him that. He would likely send for a mortal to feed me and the unfortunate person would probably never be returned to the mortal world. I would never do that. I swallowed and returned his unflinching stare. He could tell I was lying, I was certain, but he didn't argue.

Instead, I focused on him. "What were you wanting to discuss?" I asked politely.

Oddly enough, he shook his head. "Nothing really," he answered slowly, swirling the last two swallows of his nectar around in the bottom of the glass. "I just wanted to ask if you'd like to spend the night to rest. You do look weary."

I studied him for a moment, but could see nothing in his face to give away his true motive. Had he been planning to make a move on me and then had thought the better of it? I decided that was likely.

"Well, thank you for the kind thought," I replied briskly. "But it isn't necessary. I would, however, enjoy a nap before dinner."

"So be it," he nodded and then called for a servant. A tiny maid appeared at his elbow and he motioned for her to take me to a bedroom. I followed the spritely girl up the stairs. Looking back, I found Poseidon standing at the windows, looking absently out them. What a strange man.

The slight girl stopped in front of a closed door. "Here you go, miss," she curtsied. "If you need anything else, just let me know."

"Thank you," I replied, opening the bedroom door. "You're very kind." She disappeared down the hall and I entered the bedchambers.

And then I stopped in my tracks.

A girl with flame red hair was wrapped around Brennan.

# Chapter Ten

"Am I interrupting?" I asked coldly. Brennan's head flew up and his expression was astonished and dismayed. The girl stepped slowly away from him, not upset in the slightest. In fact, she looked almost pleased.

"No!" Brennan exclaimed. "Not at all, I assure you." He stepped even further away from the girl and appealed to me with his startled eyes. "I promise," he added firmly. I studied him for a brief minute and had to say, I believed him. He was certainly sincere. But the girl...

I narrowed my eyes as I focused my attention on her.

"Who are you?" I asked coldly.

She stared back at me unabashedly, even though in her enthusiasm to seduce Brennan, the straps of her flimsy gown were falling over her shoulders and she seemed half-naked as her breasts almost spilled over the top of her dress.

"I'm Adelpha," she announced proudly. "Daughter of Poseidon."

Thrusting her shoulders back, she skirted around Brennan to stand in front of me.

"And you are Empusa, daughter of the witch."

"I am Empusa, daughter of the goddess of witchcraft, yes," I snapped. "And I am a witch, as well. So. Watch. Your. Step."

My tone was ice cold and she smirked slightly, trying to appear that she was unfazed. But I could see the fear in her eyes for a scant second before she masked it. She wasn't sure what I was capable of and that made me dangerous to her. The unknown should always be considered dangerous.

"Welcome," she replied icily. "My father summoned me so that I could lead you to our island after dinner. But first, you are to rest." She gazed at me. "Clearly, you need it. You look… tired."

She turned on her heel and left the room. Brennan was at my side in a second.

"Em, I swear. I didn't do anything. She was here waiting for me. She practically attacked me. And then you walked in."

And suddenly, the reason that Poseidon had detained me became clear. He was giving his daughter a chance to seduce the son of Apollo. Perhaps he had his sights on a marriage or something to that effect. *Not going to happen, old man*, I thought grumpily, hoping that he was listening to my thoughts.

"It's alright, I believe you," I assured Brennan. "I think Poseidon sent her here to seduce you. He probably hoped you would fall in love and there could be yet another royal marriage."

"He sent his own daughter to sleep with me?" Brennan asked in astonishment.

"Brennan, seriously. When I said that this is a whole other world, I meant it. Never let your guard down, not for a moment."

He nodded. "Point taken. I've got it."

I stumbled over to the massive bed in the center of the room. I was so exhausted that I almost couldn't stand any longer.

"Are you alright?"Brennan asked in concern. "You don't look that great."

"Gee, thanks," I muttered, as I turned down the fluffy comforter and slipped inside. The sheets were cool and crisp and I had never felt anything as marvelous in my life... because I was so weary.

"Seriously," he continued as he crawled into bed next to me. "You are really pale."

"I need blood," I mumbled into my pillow. "Using my abilities so much has drained my energy. And there's no one here to replace it."

"There's me." The quiet offer caused my heart to freeze and I sat straight up in bed, although the movement took extreme effort. I was so drained that my vision was becoming blurred and that was never a good sign.

"What?" I almost whispered, trying to wrap my mind around the thought of drinking Brennan's blood. It would likely be fantastic, amazing... and that terrified me. Once I had drunk his blood, would I want any other?

"Drink mine," he offered again, shoving his sleeve up and exposing his wrist to me. "You need it, I have it. It's simply a matter of supply and demand. I don't want you to suffer- not when I can so easily help you. You won't kill me, right?"

That last part was meant as a joke, but I could see a slight bit of truth in it as I studied his face.

"No, I won't kill you," I promised as I moved toward him slowly. The room around me was starting to spin and I knew that I would have to do it. If I didn't drink Brennan's blood, I would be in serious trouble.

But what if I was in serious trouble if I *did*?

I hesitated at his side and he thrust his arm at me again.

"Do it," he insisted. "It's just a little blood. I can make more."

Just a little blood. I swallowed. I could totally do this. Couldn't I?

Bending, I steadied myself with a hand against his hard chest. I was seriously dizzy, so much so that I almost couldn't tell if I was sitting still or moving. Dipping my head, I slid my mouth along his forearm. He still smelled like sunshine, which made sense, given who he was.

My tongue inadvertently darted out and licked his skin. He tasted like sunshine, too. I sighed. There was no way around it.

Before I could change my mind, I sank my teeth into his wrist.

And then I almost died...from pleasure. Brennan's blood was the most heavenly, delectable substance on the face of the planet, better even than nectar. Aromas and tastes exploded into my mouth as every hue of the rainbow clouded my vision, blinding me. I couldn't focus on anything but the unbelievable taste. My own blood rushed through my body, pulsing hard through my limbs and causing my heart to pound so loudly I could hear it in my ears.

Through my haze, I heard him moan and knew that it was affecting him in the same way that it did every other mortal, but I couldn't focus on it even enough to be pleased. I was so involved in the moment, in how it was affecting me.

As I drank, as his vital blood gushed into my mouth and I swallowed it, allowing it to slide warmly down my throat, I realized something. His blood was tying him to me even more than he already was. I felt warmth, attachment... love.

I lifted my head incredulously. "I love you," I whispered, still astounded at the realization.

"I love you, too," he answered huskily, reaching for me. He drew me to him, covering my mouth with his own, his hands frantically sliding down my sides to my hips. "I can never be without you," he murmured against my neck. "Promise me."

I nodded, my throat almost painfully constricted. "I promise."

"Do you need more?" he asked softly, offering me his other wrist. I knew that I did. I gently broke the skin of his arm and sucked lightly, trying my best not to hurt him. From his moans of contentment, I could tell that whatever he felt, it wasn't pain.

Several moments later, my hunger was sated and I fell limply against him. He encircled me within his arms and kissed me again.

"That was… incredible. I've never felt anything like it."

"Me either," I admitted.

"Really?" he sounded surprised. "I would have thought… I mean…"

"You thought it was always like that for me?" I raised an eyebrow. "No. It's usually a method for me to eat. I don't feel a connection at all with the mortals I drink from. Except for you. I do think… I'm sure of it now… our souls are connected."

Brennan nodded. "I'm not sure what all that entails, but you must be right. What I'm feeling right now- it's wonderful and amazing- and it's not of this world. It's not normal. And I should know. I've been in love before, or so I thought. But never like this."

That statement brought me more satisfaction than I could ever have dreamed possible. He loved me more than he had ever loved anyone else. That it was so soon after we met didn't concern me at all...knowing that we were soul mates explained everything. He was the other half of my whole.

"Now what?" he asked trustingly, tracing the curve of my hip with his finger.

"Now we un-do my curse and beg Zeus for your immortality so that we can live happily ever after," I answered.

"And I thought you were going to give me a challenge," he chuckled. "This should be easy."

I rolled my eyes.

"Well, you will have to keep your hands to yourself," I muttered, envisioning Adelpha. "Do you think you can do that?"

His gaze flew to mine. "Of course. Em, I promise- I didn't do anything."

"I know," I sighed. "I'm agitated with her, not you. We should rest for a bit. Who knows where we will have to travel after dinner."

I closed my eyes and snuggled into his chest. I hated surprises.

* * *

The dinner banquet was uncomfortable, to say the least.

Poseidon sat at the head of the long elaborately adorned dining table, his face devoid of emotion as he ate his fill of shrimp, lobster and oysters. His famed trident leaned against his chair, carelessly set aside, even though it contained so much power. Although I was sure no one here would dare to touch it. Poseidon would likely cut off their hand for such an offense.

Every form of seafood imaginable was available to us and piled high on bronze platters. Brennan had dove into it with gusto, polishing off a stack of fresh crab legs. He had a small dribble of melted butter sliding down one side of his chin and I itched to lean over and wipe it away, but I didn't.

Amphitrite sat on the opposing end of the table from Poseidon and she barely smiled throughout the dinner. It was very apparent to anyone who looked at her that she was unhappy. Her mouth was drawn and pinched, her eyes devoid of joy. I had to imagine that life with the god of the sea was hardly joyful.

Regardless of the beautiful furnishings, the atmosphere was stiff and tense here and I had a feeling it was the same whenever Poseidon was in attendance. He was certainly a very stern person and his brooding presence carried throughout the room.

Brennan kicked me under the table and I looked at him, raising my eyebrow.

"What's going on here?" he whispered. "When can we leave?"

Apparently, he hadn't learned his lesson about god hearing. Every head at the table turned to us and Poseidon practically impaled him with his glare.

"Are you in such a hurry, young pup, to leave my safekeeping?"

The room was as silent as a tomb as everyone waited for Brennan to answer. I interrupted before he could say anything even more foolish.

"Of course not, Poseidon," I assured him. "It's just that Brennan is unaccustomed to the ways of the gods. He has much to learn and I fear it makes him uncomfortable."

I felt Brennan's appreciative gaze as Poseidon nodded, appeased. "I can imagine," he nodded. "Things are much different here than with the mortal heathens."

Everyone around us nodded in agreement, whether they truly agreed or simply wanted to please Poseidon, I didn't know.

I brought another spoon of lobster chowder to my lips as Brennan appraised me. He smiled a small smile and I knew that he was thinking about earlier… when he had truly appeased my hunger. Thoughts of that experience flushed my cheeks and Poseidon caught my eye.

"You look much better now, Empusa," he observed. "You are not nearly so pale. I trust that your nap worked well for you."

I nodded, as I swallowed my soup. "Yes, thank you," I replied politely, deciding I had to change the subject quickly.

"I must admit that I share Brennan's anxiety about our destination. After running from my father for so long, it will be nice to relax and not have to constantly look over my shoulder. Thank you again for you hospitality and willingness to help me. May I ask where you will be taking us?"

Poseidon leaned back in his seat and a faraway look glazed his eyes over. "Ah," he replied. "I will be hiding you away in my favorite place in the world."

I waited, but he didn't continue. It was as if he felt I should know where his favorite place was.

"Where is that?" Brennan asked curiously. Poseidon eyed him impatiently, slamming his nectar goblet down onto the table with enough force that nectar splashed onto the linen table cloth.

"Atlantis, foolish child. Where else?"

As soon as Poseidon said the words, they made perfect sense. Of course- Atlantis. It was the lost, sunken city- the mortals certainly couldn't find it and Poseidon had enchanted it just as he had enchanted the city we were currently in. It was a city of gold and silver and unimaginable beauty. I had never personally been there, but I had heard many stories of it through the years.

"Atlantis is real?" Brennan raised an eyebrow and the entire table erupted into laughter. He flushed and glanced at me sheepishly. He truly did have many things to learn.

"Of course it is, son of Apollo," Amphitrite soothed him as she pushed away from the table. "It is where Poseidon keeps his most treasured possession."

The table stilled. I could hear rasping breaths and heartbeats.

"And what is that?" Brennan asked hesitantly, because it was clear that Amphitrite wanted him to. She was waiting for it and so was everyone else. I sighed because I already knew the answer.

"His mistress," she snapped, glaring at her husband before she turned on her heel and stalked away. The entire table stayed frozen until she had disappeared from sight and then normal activity resumed once more as though nothing had happened.

I couldn't help but giggle at Brennan's astounded gaze. He had so much to learn. So many of the gods had mistresses, lovers, hidden agendas. There were a few that were loyal and true, but I could count them on one hand.

"Someday, you'll meet Harmonia and Cadmus," I told Brennan quietly, changing the subject. "They are quite normal and you'll like them. They are completely devoted to each other and you'll never meet a lovelier person than Harmonia."

"And they are?"

"They are our saviors!" Poseidon snapped, his eyes crackling. "Do you know nothing of your own history!?"he boomed.

I rushed to soothe him. "My apologies again, Poseidon. I have not fully explained everything to Brennan. And as you know, since those events were so recent, they have not made it into mortal history books."

"Mortals do not believe in us anymore, anyway," a child down the table chimed in. I glanced down at her. She was right and more was the pity.

"Why don't you do something to change that?" Brennan asked, switching his gaze from Poseidon and then back to me. The god of the sea looked at Brennan as though he had lost his mind.

"Why should we care?" he asked humorlessly. "The mortals are of little consequence to us. We go on about our lives, they go on about theirs. We all serve our purpose. It matters not if they believe or do not believe."

I shook my head. Poseidon really had a negative outlook on life.

"As I was saying about Harmonia and Cadmus," I turned my attention back to Brennan. "They are a breath of fresh air. She is the goddess of contentment and peace and it is true. She saved all of the Olympians, including my mother. Hades and the Fates had imprisoned them in the Underworld and she fought to free them. She lives there now, with her husband Cadmus and their little girl Raquel. They live in a fascinating replica of Olympus in the Isles of the Blessed. Perhaps you will meet them when they are visiting the Spiritlands."

"You will depart for Atlantis as soon as you are finished eating," Poseidon thundered and strode from the room.

Brennan and I looked at each other. "What the hell was that about?" he asked incredulously. "Was it something we said?"

The little girl who had spoken earlier piped up again. "Do not worry, son of Apollo. My papa explodes like that fairly often. My mama says he has a horrible temper. He doesn't like to talk about Harmonia. Mama says it is because he's embarrassed that he allowed himself to get trapped by Uncle Hades."

I smiled at her. "Thank you, little one. We shall try to not let it alarm us, then."

She nodded and continued munching on her fish. Brennan made quick work of the rest of his plate and we sat silently, waiting to see what would happen. We didn't have to wait long. Within a few minutes, Adelpha appeared in the doorway.

She was dressed in a floor length white satin gown, skin tight and with a slit to her thigh. Her flaming crimson hair was piled on her head and her green eyes sparkled becomingly, perfectly accented by a thick emerald necklace and earrings. I couldn't deny that she was a beautiful girl.

"Are you ready?" she asked us pleasantly, her eyes fixed on Brennan.

He nodded. "We're so... underdressed. Are we attending something formal?"

She shook her head as she laughed, a tinkling sound not unlike breaking glass.

"Of course not, darling. I just like to dress up for guests."

"Yeah, guests of the male persuasion, "I muttered beneath my breath. Brennan glanced at me, laughter in his eyes. Apparently, he was learning to hone his supernatural hearing. He laughed and then helped me from my seat.

"We're ready when you are," he told Adelpha, his hand on my arm.

"Then come with me," she purred, slinking to his side and grasping his other arm. "Trust me, you're going to enjoy this," she whispered into his ear. I sighed as we walked from the room.

# Chapter Eleven

Atlantis was magnificent.

I stood from the balcony of our room and stared out at the expanse of city sprawled in front of me. It was absolutely, breathtakingly incredible. Like the rest of Poseidon's underwater kingdom, it was encased in a strange invisible bubble, protecting it from the depths of waters above it.

It was quiet and colorful with bronzes, golds and silvers glinting in the watery light. Exquisite, brightly colored homes lined the streets, well-dressed civilians bustled here and there, perfectly manicured flowers and plants adorned the walkways. It was truly a sanctuary and it was no wonder that it was Poseidon's favorite place in the world.

His mistress, Cleito, oversaw the palace here and she was as beautiful and bubbly as Amphitrite was plain and mousy. It was clear why Poseidon preferred to be here, rather than there.

"What are you thinking?"

Brennan emerged from the adjoining sitting room of our suite and rubbed my shoulders, leaning around me to kiss my cheek softly. I still felt sizzling jolts of electricity when he touched me, but I had learned to handle it… and enjoy it.

"I'm marveling at the beauty here," I admitted, turning to face him. "I thought I had seen everything… the Spiritlands, the Underworld and everything in between. But Atlantis… well, Atlantis rivals all of it."

"Agreed," Brennan replied, staring past me at the beautiful scenery over my shoulder. "I've never seen those other places, but it is hard to imagine that there is anything in the world that is more beautiful than here. Except for maybe you."

He shifted his gaze again, this time to stare into my eyes. I was mesmerized once again by the flecks of amber and gold within the warm depths of his. No wonder Adelpha was interested. Brennan was as breathtaking as our view.

"Thank you," he grinned and I scowled. I had forgotten, once again, that he was mastering his abilities and could read my mind. He had heard my unspoken compliment.

"So, what do we do now?" he asked seriously, rubbing my forearm slightly.

"I'm not sure," I admitted. "I think we probably should wait here until I hear from my mother. Supposedly, it isn't safe for me to go to her. Something must be going on that I don't know about yet."

"Hmm. So we have to hang out in paradise and get to know each other," Brennan sighed melodramatically. "I don't know if I can handle this punishment."

"As long as part of your punishment doesn't include Adelpha, we'll be okay," I warned him, only half joking. I didn't like this other side of me, this jealous, slightly insecure side. But I had never felt such strong feelings for someone before. I was still processing how to handle it.

"Sweetheart, she doesn't even begin to compare to you," Brennan reassured me, lifting my hand to kiss it lightly. As his warm lips brushed my fingers, a tingle ran down my spine and I shivered. He stared at me, waiting.

"And now would be the time where you said that no one can compare to me, either," he prompted.

I smiled. It was good to know that he needed assurances from me, as well. This whole soul mate thing had apparently caught us both off guard.

"It's true," I told him with a grin. "No one can compare to you. Not the earth, not the sun, not Zeus himself."

He glared at me. "Not exactly the sincere, heartfelt moment I was looking for."

"Okay, okay. I'm serious now. There is only you. From the moment I saw you, I knew it. No one else in the entire world can compare to what I feel for you." I smiled. "Is that better?"

"Much," he smirked, apparently appeased. He dragged me to him and kissed me gently. "I love you,

you know. Don't laugh. I feel like I've known you for a thousand years."

"You have no idea what a thousand years is," I replied. "But I do. And trust me, I wish I'd been with you for each one of them. It feels unfair that we've only just found each now, like all of that other time was wasted. But we have eternity together now."

He looked uncertain. "Only if Zeus will allow it."

I nodded. "True. Only if Zeus will allow it. But I think I know how to manage that."

Brennan looked interested. "Do tell, shortcake."

"Harmonia. Remember the story that I told you-about how she saved the Olympians? That includes Zeus. He owes her… huge. And she happens to owe me, too. Sort of."

"How is that?" he wrinkled his brow. "I thought I heard someone at the table whispering that she was the Chosen One or something like that. How does the Chosen One owe you?"

"Don't look so surprised!" I swatted him on the arm. "When I was still in the Underworld, I found her daughter before she did. I kept Raquel safe until Harmonia could find us. I just know that if we asked her to plead your case to Zeus, she would. Technically, she has already repaid her debt. She chose to stay in the Underworld so that I could leave. But I just know that if I asked her for help, she would give it. She knows what it is like to love someone and lose them. I have faith that she wouldn't want to wish that on me."

"That sounds like a great plan," he nodded. "But first we have to handle this mess that you're in. We can secure my immortality later. I can't even believe I just said that," he shook his head. "A few days ago, I would have never believed any of this. I was just a normal guy, living in a normal town, going to a normal school, dating normal girls. I was going to be a dentist, you know. And then I met you. And now nothing will ever be the same."

"Well, you certainly won't need to be a dentist," I chuckled. "And I'll just tell you right now that I'm not a 'normal girl'."

He threw back his head and laughed, a sound so rich that it seemed like melted chocolate drizzled in caramel and honey.

"No," he agreed quickly, soaking me in his sunny gaze. "You are most certainly not a normal girl. But compared to you, normal girls are boring. Very, very boring."

"Well," I gave him the once over. "I do come with baggage. Wouldn't you rather not have a crazy, psychopath chasing you?"

He pretended to consider that, cocking his head thoughtfully. "Perhaps. But the benefits outweigh the negatives. It's sort of nice that you can conjure anything from thin air. And you're kind of cute, too."

I raised an eyebrow. "Would you like to explore Atlantis or stand here and continue to flatter me so smoothly?"

He seemed outraged. "What? My silver tongue isn't working on you?"

"Hardly. I've heard better compliments coming from a third grader. But I'll forgive you- because you're kind of cute, too. Shall we explore?"

He eyed me for a minute before shrugging and sticking out his arm. "Sure. I don't have anything else to do."

I cocked an eyebrow and he laughed.

"Of course I would love to explore with you," he rephrased with a smile.

I took his arm and we strolled from the palace out to the front grounds. It was absolutely incredible. The scents of roses and hyacinths filled the air around us as we walked slowly down the manicured paths. We got some curious stares, but no one spoke to us. Everyone around us seemed to have a purpose, as though they had jobs to do and places to go.

"Can I be honest?" Brennan asked me.

"Of course," I replied. "I expect nothing less."

"I sort of feel like I fell down a rabbit hole. This is all so... crazy."

I nodded. "I can only imagine what it must be like for you. This craziness has always been my life, so I've never had to absorb it like you have. But you've handled it so well. Truly- I'm really impressed."

"Well, thank you," he grinned. I doubted that I would ever get tired of seeing his smile. It lit up my heart. "Can I tell you something else?"

I glanced at him. "Sure. I guess."

"There's nothing I would rather do than march you back up to our room and stay there. For days."

His grin was suggestive now and so, so sexy. My knees felt weak.

"I...uh. You know we can't," I finally managed to get out. "It's too dangerous. We have to be careful until this curse is reversed. I don't want to lose control and accidentally take your soul."

He looked unconcerned. "Even if, worst case scenario, you sucked down my soul. Zeus can un-do anything right? I mean, he's the god of all gods."

I stared at him. Was he serious?

"You only have one soul," I reminded him seriously. "We have to protect it- even from me. Especially from me. Zeus can't always fix things- it depends on what else it effects and so on. We can't take that chance. So until then, hands off, buddy."

I smiled to take the sting out of my words, but the implication was still there. We had to maintain a careful distance from each other. It was the responsible thing to do.

"Fine," he smiled a slow purposeful smile, the kind that instantly made me nervous. "I'll be good. If you will."

Gulp. He had me there. I was struggling with it just as much as he was.

"Fine," I agreed stoutly, determined not to let my hesitation shine through. I could so do this. "I heard they have their very own sea of tranquility down here. Would you like to go look at it?"

"And be all tranquil and stuff?" he cocked an eyebrow. "Sure. Sounds peaceful."

I laughed. I had to admit, I adored his sense of humor. I would rather have a great sense of humor in a man over good-looks any day. Luckily with Brennan, I didn't have to choose. He had them both.

"Fine. Let's go get our peace on."

We wound our way around the beautiful, glistening city and after being pointed in the right direction by a friendly shopkeeper, we finally found the shimmering sea. It was amazing. Simply standing beside it, I felt a wave of calm descend over me. No wonder they called it the sea of tranquility. It apparently had calming powers.

"Is this the way it is always going to be?" Brennan asked as he stared across the rippling waters. "Will there always be something magical or fantastic around the next corner for me to stumble upon?"

"Yes," I confirmed. "There is always something fantastical around every bend when you are dealing with the gods. The mortal world... well, it simply can't prepare you for this. You'll still be learning about our world a hundred years from now. It is always changing."

"I figured as much," he sighed. "But at least I have a beautiful tour guide."

He grabbed my hand and we stood quietly observing the beauty around us. But strangely enough, it didn't remain still. The water began swirling, like a magnificent whirlpool.

"What's happening?" Brennan asked curiously as we kept our eyes glued to the churning sea.

"I'm not sure," I answered uncertainly.

The water was moving quickly now, swirling into an inverted funnel, lifting from the sea itself and towards the sky.

"What the…"I breathed.

And then the water took shape, moving into the form of an old, stooped woman. She took a watery step towards us, skimming across the top of the sea until she stood directly in front of us, glistening in the light.

And then she materialized.

"Circes," I muttered.

My mother's old crony, Circes, stooped in front of us, her long black skirts fluttering around her in the wind. She was gnarled and ancient, her white, straggly hair trailing down her crooked back. She had been a friend of my mother's for a very long time.

Her faded eyes met mine and just for a second, I saw something in hers. Fear. My breath escaped my lips in a rush. I had never, in my life, seen Circes afraid. The old woman was fearless.

"What is it?"I asked her quickly, stepping forward to grasp her arm gently. "Is something wrong with my mother?"

Circes smiled, her yellowed teeth twisting into a grotesque grin. "Of course not, child. Your mother is able to handle herself, more so than anyone else that I know. I'm here at her bidding, princess."

She dropped her head slightly in deference to me. Witches often referred to me as the Princess of the Moon, although to be honest, I most certainly didn't feel like a princess. No other princess that I knew of had to run for her life.

"And what does she wish for you to do, Circes?" I asked politely, hoping that my impatience was masked by my friendly tone. The sea breeze whipped at my hair and I brushed it back. As I did, Brennan swept his hand along my back, presumably as a sign of support. I glanced at him in appreciation.

I hadn't realized how alone I truly had been until now. It was nice to have someone on my side...someone who was with me no matter what. My heart swelled at the thought and I forced myself to focus on Circes.

"Well?" I prompted her. "What message does she send you with?"

She smiled again and appraised me with her eerie faded eyes. By all appearances, she should be blind. But she could still see. It was unnerving.

"Your mother knows that you have drunk from the boy's blood- the son of Apollo," she uttered.

"And?" I raised my eyebrow. Brennan's thumb rubbed a circle on my back and I found myself leaning into his hand, leaning into his warmth. It felt like a connection and I enjoyed it.

"And she wishes to offer you a warning. She has spoken to you about the nature of moonlight, yes?" It was Circes' turn to raise her thin eyebrow. I nodded.

"Yes."

"Moonlight is only a reflection of the sun," she reiterated needlessly. "Do not allow the boy to drink from your blood. You don't understand the power that you could unleash. It is unlikely that you would be able to control it."

Brennan's hand froze, as did the breath in my throat. "Why would I allow Brennan to drink from my blood?" I managed to squeak. "He is not a blood drinker. He's mortal."

"For now," Circes acknowledged. "Just heed the warning, princess. Your mother felt it was important enough to send me here, so it must be important indeed."

I nodded. "You may tell my mother that I understand," I instructed. "But I do not understand why my mother did not come herself. She is not afraid of anything. Why is she hiding?"

Circes examined me, reading my face like a book before her gaze flitted back to my eyes. Hers were filled with wisdom and concern.

"Hecate does not hide," she announced proudly. "And she is never afraid. The only thing Hecate fears is losing you. You are her one weakness. And that is why she sent me."

"Well, that's vague," Brennan muttered quietly. Circes' ancient eyes snapped in Brennan's direction.

"Do you have something to say, son of Apollo?" she snapped. I couldn't understand the dislike in her voice. She had never even met Brennan, much less have had any opportunity in which he could have offended her. He must have shared my thought.

"Have I done something to you?" he asked her firmly. "I've never met you before, so I find it hard to believe that I have wronged you in any way."

Circes pursed her lips together and rocked back on her heels, her black heavy skirt swirling around her gnarled bare feet.

"You have not purposely offended me, it is true," she admitted grudgingly. "But your presence, your life itself, threatens my princess. And that offends me."

Brennan froze, as did I.

"What do you mean?" he asked slowly. "How do I threaten Empusa?"

"We have seen it!" Circes hissed, her ancient face contorting in her agitation. "Empusa will risk everything for you. What we cannot see… is if she survives."

# Chapter Twelve

Brennan and I sat quietly in our suite while we faced each other on the bed. We were so still that when a tiny muscle in my foot twinged, I jumped in surprise. The tension was so palpable, I could practically breathe it in. Brennan reached out and grasped my hand, stroking my fingers with his.

"I won't hurt you, Em," he assured me quietly. "If it means that I need to leave you and return to the mortal world, I'll do that. I couldn't stand it if something happened to you because of me. I would rather die."

The mere thought of Brennan leaving caused my heart to flutter uncontrollably in my chest. The thought of his death, even uttered as a casual comment, made me physically sick.

"Don't be ridiculous!" I exclaimed, clutching his hand and bringing it to my chest, holding it against my thudding heart. "It will be fine. I don't know what Circes meant, but it doesn't matter."

"It does matter," he insisted. "She said that you will risk everything for me."

Brennan's eyes were liquid topaz and I had the sudden thought that I might fall into them and drown.

The angles of his face distracted me and I reached out with tentative fingers and traced his cheekbone.

"It will be fine," I murmured, leaning in to kiss the side of his neck against my better judgment. I was usually the temptress, the one that men found irresistible. But with Brennan, the shoe was on the other foot. That I tempted him was indisputable, but he tempted me just as much.

Brennan closed his eyes and I ran my nose along his skin. For the first time in days, I felt the need to inhale him and my fingers started to shake. I started to pull away but he held me firm.

"You'll be fine," he assured me, staring into my eyes. "You won't hurt me."

"Brennan…" my voice trailed off and I swallowed. "Don't be so confident in me. I don't *want* to hurt you. But there's a big difference between what I want and what I might actually do."

"Remember?" he asked gently. "I can see the future sometimes. And I can see you in mine. That must mean that A). You don't kill me and B). We're together. And those are the only two things that matter, right?"

My eyes flew to his face.

"You've seen our future?" I asked hesitantly, dropping my hands to my lap.

He nodded solemnly.

"Yes."

Long pause.

"And?" I demanded impatiently.

He picked my hand back up. "I can't see the details. It's blurry- as though I'm looking through fog. But I can see you in it, I can see me in it and we're together. I see you holding my hand. And that's good, right?"

"That depends," I replied cautiously. "How far in the future are you seeing?"

"I can't tell," he shrugged. "But I can tell that it's a while. Why are you so curious? You've already told me- once you're immortal, time is nothing."

He seemed unconcerned.

"That is true," I acknowledged. "Usually. But our current situation is tenuous at best. It would be nice to know if it all turns out alright."

"It will," he nodded. "I'm going to concentrate on willing it so."

"Oh, really?" I laughed, breaking the tension. "You're going to 'will' it so? Well, why didn't you say so earlier? I wouldn't have worried."

"You doubt me?" he cocked an eyebrow and then pushed me over onto the cushiony pillows. "I know what I'm talking about," he said smugly as he tucked a stray piece of hair behind my ear.

"Then why, pray tell, were you worried two seconds ago about my future, if you're already convinced that you can 'will' it into being wonderful?" I asked.

His face clouded and I instantly wished I could take back the words. He'd been distracted and I'd ruined it. I mentally kicked myself.

"I know," he mumbled. "I'm worried because futures can change. What I see today might not be the same thing tomorrow- any number of factors could influence it, change it. That's why I will work so hard to try to will it into what we want."

Once again, my heart melted at his words. He was trying so hard. He had been thrust into such a strange new world and he had embraced it...mainly for me. I gulped.

"It will be fine," I said quietly. "We'll be together, so whatever comes, it will be fine. I love you, Brennan."

He stared at me, quietly and with his face bathed in light from the window.

"I love you, too," he replied gently, cupping my face in his hands, before he lowered his to mine. "Everything will be fine," he murmured against my lips.

He didn't sound as sure of himself now as he did and I felt horrible. I had done that. My doubt had taken his hope.

"I'm serious," I told him. "My mother is on our side and I can assure you that there is no one that you'd rather have on your side than the goddess of witchcraft."

He smiled. "I can only imagine. And I can't wait to meet her, by the way. In the mortal world, it is customary for potential husbands to gain the father's approval but in this case, I think we'd better skip that part." He smiled, but I found it hard to breathe.

"Husband?" My voice was suddenly tiny in the huge suite.

He looked surprised. "I just assumed that you would want to marry me. I'm sorry. Do you not?"

I couldn't help it. I burst into laughter. "That was the most un-romantic proposal that I've ever heard," I gasped as I held my sides and tried to breathe. Brennan looked indignant and offended, sticking his roman nose into the air.

"Well, I take it back then," he sniffed. "I don't want to marry you after all."

He crossed his arms over his chest and acted like he was pouting.

"Really?" I crawled toward him on all fours and then plunked into his lap, ignoring his whoosh of air as I knocked the breath out of him. "Because I think that the idea has merit."

"You do?" he couldn't help but bite. I smiled.

"Because I might consider it," I nibbled his bottom lip. "If we make it out of this alive."

He froze and then relaxed. "You like to shock me," he observed. "I'll need to get used to that."

I laughed and curled up on his chest, allowing my eyelids to close. A nap might work wonders for my mood. Brennan's arms wrapped around me were strong and warm and I concentrated on the rhythmic rise and fall of his chest as I let the blackness of sleep overtake me.

* * *

I was cold. It took me a moment to realize that someone was invading the peacefulness of my sleep, that their presence was causing a chill. Whispers surrounded me, hissing and dark. Cold tendrils of smoke curled around my shoulders like frigid fingers and I frantically looked around, trying to see who had stolen into my head. A foreboding sensation was pressing downward onto my chest, crushing it.

"Hello, daughter."

The voice hissed from shadows and I struggled to see him.

Him.

Mormo.

*My father.*

"How did you get in here?" I called out. "My dreams are supposed to be safe from you. My mind is protected."

"Protected by what?" he mocked me. "A spell? I know your mother better than anyone, better than you. It only takes me so long to figure out what she's done to protect you and undo her spells. Nice bracelet, by the way."

My gaze flew to my wrist where my enchanted bracelet should be. But of course it wasn't now. It was in Poseidon's pocket.

"What did you do?" I snapped.

Mormo finally stepped out of the smoky shadows and I sucked a deep breath in to steady my nerves. He was an ominous presence, scary and large. His hawkish face was gaunt and white, his dark hair severe against his pale skin.

*He can't hurt me here.*

*He can't hurt me here.*

*He can't hurt me here.*

"Can't I?" he asked softly, his teeth glistening in the muted light of my dream as he read my thoughts.

"No, you can't," I answered sharply. "You can't. What have I ever done to you to deserve what you have done?"

Satisfaction rose in my chest, a delicious feeling. I had never been able to face him before- to demand answers. I realized in this instant how unsettling that had been. I deserved answers. I deserved closure.

"It's never been about you," he answered in disgust. "Why are you so self-centered? Your goddess blood shows itself. *Everything is not about you.*"

He practically spit his last sentence and I recoiled from the venom in his tone.

"If it's not about me, then why do you hate me so much?" I whispered. "I'm your daughter- your own blood. But you would kill me if you could. How could I not take that personally?"

His smile grew wider, like a wolf's, and I once again drew away from him.  He approached me, moving as quietly and quickly as the wind.  I could feel his breath on my cheek, on my neck, as he glided to a stop behind me.

"It's not personal," he breathed into my ear, his voice like ice.  "But I will kill you.  I have to. It's the only way I can survive."

"So it's you or me, then?"

I whirled to face him, backing away once again.  I knew he couldn't hurt me here. But that didn't put me at ease.

"I'm glad you understand." His gray eyes, just like mine, glittered menacingly. My heart, even though I had always protected it from him, seemed to wither just a little at the knowledge that my own father hated me so much.

"I don't hate you," he answered my thought.  "You aren't anything to me."

Another piece of my heart dried up and I tried to harden myself against him.

"Why are you here?" I snapped. "What do you want to say to me if I'm nothing to you?"

"Oh, nothing," he replied casually, his hands dropping to his sides.  "I just thought I would check in on you."

"And offer me a warning?" My words were like icy arrows aimed at his heart, but I should have known they would fall impotent to the ground. He didn't have one.

He laughed, a chilling sound in the bleakness of my nightmare. "Perhaps," he conceded with a nod. "And perhaps I just wanted to distract you."

The icy tendrils grasping my shoulders slipped to my stomach, gripping it tightly.

"Distract me?" I whispered, not comprehending. "From what?"

"And what fun would I glean from simply telling you?" he asked humorlessly. "It will be ever so much more satisfying to watch you discover it for yourself."

"Discover it..." my voice trailed off as I studied his satisfied expression. What had he done?

Realization hit me like a ton of bricks.

Brennan.

My heart raced and my vision blurred as I struggled to wake.

*Wake up.*

*Wake up.*

*Wake up.*

My eyes popped open and I gasped for air, trying to breathe, to make sense of what had just happened. And as I did, I realized something. I was cold. I was cold when I shouldn't be because Brennan was very, very warm. I had fallen asleep to his warmth. I glanced around me. My bed was very, very empty.

"Brennan!" I screamed, my voice shrill and fragile as I leapt from the bed and blurred with inhuman velocity toward the door.

Our suite was empty.

The hall outside of our suite was empty.

"Brennan!" I screeched again, flying down the empty corridors of Poseidon's palace as fast as I could move.

"Stop!" Poseidon roared from the other end of the hall. I slid to a stop in front of him, certain that I was as wild-eyed as a crazy woman.

"Where's Brennan?" I cried. "Something's wrong."

"Brennan left," Poseidon answered calmly, his hands on his hips as he filled the corridor. "He insisted."

"What?" I shrieked. "Why? He wouldn't leave me."

Poseidon shrugged and blew into his hand, then opened his palm and blew again in my direction. A puff of filmy mist floated in my direction. A memory.

I leaned forward and inhaled it, tossing my head back like I was swallowing a pill.

Instantly, Brennan filled my mind as clearly as if he were standing in front of me. I reached out with shaking fingers, but of course he wasn't really there and my fingers clenched at empty air.

"I have to leave!" he begged someone, presumably Poseidon. "If I stay, she will die."

"She can't die," Poseidon answered, his voice bored. "She's immortal."

"Listen to me," Brennan pleaded. "Please. Her mother came to me in a dream. Apparently, Mormo can shape-shift. He appeared to Empusa as Ahmose, an old ancient. Mormo's the one who led us here. Empusa's not safe here. I have to find her mother."

Poseidon's laugh boomed and I shrank away from the tone. He was pleased with himself. Why?

Brennan's eyes narrowed suspiciously. "Why do you laugh?" he asked.

"Why do you speak to me as if you're telling me something that I didn't already know?" Poseidon countered. "Of course I knew it was Mormo. And of course I know that it isn't safe for Empusa here. It's my kingdom, after all. I know everything."

A chill settled onto me and I snapped out of his memory and into the present, staring into Poseidon's silver eyes.

"Why?" I whispered. "Why have you betrayed me?"

He smiled patiently. "Mormo paid the highest price," he explained with a shrug. "It's nothing personal."

It was the second time in a space of five minutes that I had heard that line. And it still felt very, very personal.

# Chapter Thirteen

"Where did Brennan go?" I demanded, unafraid of the god of the sea. Poseidon seemed amused at my impertinence, as I stood facing him with my hands on my hips.

"He left for the mortal world, of course," Poseidon answered with a smile.

"You let him leave?" I was fairly astonished.

"Why would I not?" Poseidon asked, his amusement apparent. "I wish him gone. We only wanted you."

"We?" I was scared to know… but I had to.

"Yes, we," he confirmed. "Your father and me."

My heart stilled.

"Why are you working with my father? He's a hateful, horrible person. He would stab you in the back as quick as he would look at you. I should know."

Poseidon nodded. "I know. But your father… he certainly knows how to pitch something. The deal he offered was very attractive, too attractive to turn down."

My words froze in my throat and I struggled to swallow past them as they formed a heavy lump. Fear turned to ice in my stomach and my heart raced as I finally managed to speak.

"What deal did he offer? What has he done to me this time?" My voice was calm and cold and didn't portray the terror that was coursing through my veins. I allowed myself some pride for that Herculean act.

Poseidon stared at me, his silver eyes rippling as he thought. "He told me of your Moonstone."

My Moonstone. I tried to act nonchalant, but inside, I was quaking. How had I forgotten? They had tricked me into giving it to Poseidon in exchange for his safekeeping. That was a joke now. I forced my lip not to curl.

"What of it?" I asked coolly. "It was enchanted to protect me from my father. You have it now."

Poseidon unconsciously patted the side of his cloak where, presumably, he had stashed my bracelet. "That I do, princess," he murmured. "But obviously that is the least of the Moonstone's powers."

I couldn't keep the surprise off of my face, but I quickly masked it as I remembered something. When my mother had first given me the bracelet, she had told me that it had other powers... powers that we could discuss 'later'. We never had a chance and I had forgotten. The most important thing on my mind was survival and the bracelet had served its purpose in that. Until now. Until I had willingly given it away. I cringed at the thought.

"Oh, sweet princess," Poseidon said softly, moving to my side and running a long, cold finger down my cheek. "Why the gloom? I won't hurt you."

"Yet," I said through gritted teeth as I drew away from his cold hand. I could feel his chilling presence directly behind me as I turned. He seemed almost amphibious and I wondered if, as the god of the sea, that was exactly the case.

"You won't hurt me," I clarified. "You'll just turn me over to my father- who will kill me with a smile."

"But I won't watch," Poseidon promised. "Does that make a difference?"

"Not really," I snapped. "I'll still be dead whether you watch or not. My mother will come for you. You know that, right?"

A brief flash of something- fear?- flashed over his face, but Poseidon quickly masked it.

"I am the god of the sea," he boomed. "I fear no one." He drew his arm back as though he were going to slap me, but didn't. After a moment, he dropped his arm to his side.

"You fear no one but your brother Zeus and my mother," I corrected stonily. "And with good reason. My mother will track you to the ends of the earth if you allow any harm to come to me."

"I'm not afraid of your mother," Poseidon insisted, but it wasn't convincing. All of the Olympians had a healthy respect for my mother, with good reason.

"As you say," I said agreeably, knowing full well that it was a lie. "Where is Mormo? When shall I die?"

I thought I sounded stunningly calm, considering my circumstances. I clenched my fists to keep them from shaking and betraying my fear.

"He's gone to track your boyfriend," Poseidon replied pleasantly. Panic lurched into my chest once again.

"He's tracking Brennan? Why?"

"After seeing the two of you together, he's got a crazy idea that you and Apollo's son have a strong connection- as strong as his and Hecate's. If you are true soul mates, then Mormo thinks that he can strengthen the power of the Moonstone even further."

My worry for Brennan was clouded by confusion. "Why is the Moonstone so important to you?" I asked. "What important powers does it hold?"

Poseidon studied me thoughtfully once again, stroking his chiseled chin. "You truly do not know?" he asked. "I find that difficult to believe."

"I have nothing to gain by lying at this juncture," I replied with my chin stuck out. "I truly do not know the extent of my Moonstone's powers. I only used it as a protective charm. All that has ever mattered to me was staying safe."

"And see where that landed you," Poseidon observed humorlessly. "I find that I am not enjoying this as much as I had envisioned, little witch princess. I am almost regretful. But not quite."

"Of course not," I said wryly under my breath. "So, since you are not regretful, what will you do with me?"

I did a remarkable job of simply sounding interested rather than afraid.

Poseidon didn't answer. Instead, he grabbed my wrist and dragged me behind him as he blurred into motion and flew down the corridor. We spiraled down the staircases of the palace until we were in the bowels, the musty dampness all around us.

He stopped in the middle of a darkened room, bare except for the stone floor itself. Chains and manacles were hanging from the ceiling and I knew that we were in the dungeon. I looked around warily.

"What are we doing here?" I asked quietly.

Moisture dripped from the ceiling onto the stones next to me and I shivered from the cold.

"Welcome to your new room," Poseidon said, as if he was welcoming me to the Beverly Wilshire hotel. "I do hope you enjoy your stay."

I stared at him for a moment before I yanked my arm from his grasp.

"Get away from me!" I hissed, hurling him across the room with goddess strength. He wasn't expecting it, so he hadn't braced himself. He crashed into the stone wall and bounced back up with the agility of a lion.

He circled me, his silver eyes glittering.

"Now, now, Empusa," he murmured, his voice dangerous. "Is that any way to treat your host?"

"You can't keep me here!" I tossed my head haughtily, blurring toward the door. Before I had taken two steps, though, Poseidon spoke.

"Stop."

The word was quiet, almost so quiet that I couldn't hear it. But I found that once he had spoken it, I was literally not able to lift my feet again to walk. It was as if they were bound to the floor with invisible cables. I glanced around in confusion and found Poseidon holding my bracelet, smiling patiently.

"What have you done?" I whispered.

"Oh, I haven't done anything," he argued politely. "It was your mother. Did she never tell you? The same enchantment used to protect you, when held in the wrong hands, can be used to control you. Minor detail."

Minor detail. I swallowed hard and took a steadying breath. Poseidon watched in pleasure.

"I would have thought that Hecate would have explained that to you. She should have told you to never let the bracelet out of your sight."

She had. She had told me to never take the bracelet off. She hadn't mentioned why. That would have been a good detail to know.

Poseidon read my face. "Ah. She did warn you. It is interesting that you didn't heed your mother's advice. She's a very wise woman."

He clutched my bracelet in his hand, stroking the smooth face of the moonstone with his other fingers.

"Come to me, Empusa," he commanded.

I couldn't disobey. My feet practically moved on their own accord. I tried to stop, to force them to still, but it was like trying to stop a moving train. My traitorous body moved to a smooth stop in front of the god of the sea.

Poseidon's chiseled features were pleased and rock hard as he appraised me, his cold gaze stroking me from top to bottom. It was almost as if he was touching me. I shuddered.

"I could save you," he stated emotionlessly, as though he didn't truly care one way or the other.

"At what price?" I asked, almost afraid to know, my breath hitching in my throat. His grin stretched evilly.

"All you would need to do would be to stay with me," he suggested. "Stay here in my underwater world."

I sucked in my breath. Stay here?

"But I don't want to," I almost stuttered, my words feeling wooden on my tongue. "I don't wish to be here."

"You know," Poseidon pondered. "I'm not known for giving a woman's wishes much weight. I'll give you until tomorrow morning to change your mind willingly. After that, I could- if I chose- command you to stay."

He held up my bracelet as a reminder. He could control my every move. My head and shoulders slumped in defeat. What chance did I have now?

"Think about it overnight," he instructed softly, leaning over to kiss my lips. His were cold and hard. I felt like I was kissing a Great White shark. "The tables have turned, haven't they, Empusa? You're so accustomed to being the dangerous one. And now you are helpless. Have a good night."

With a swirl of his cloak, he was gone. The metal door clanged loudly behind him and I heard a key turn in the lock. I flew to the door and pounded on it, kicked at it with every ounce of my considerable strength, but it didn't budge.

In my head, I heard Poseidon's voice. *Don't resist. Resistance is futile.*

In response to his unspoken command, my arms dropped to my sides. I screamed in frustration- in my mind- but nothing came from lips. I was helpless here. I was simply a puppet with invisible strings.

I leaned against the cold stone wall and slid to the ground. I knew that the rough stone was scratching my back, but I didn't care. By this time tomorrow, I would either be dead by Mormo's hand or an unwilling sex slave to the god of the sea. Neither of those options were appealing, although out of the two, I would actually rather be dead.

I sighed and laid on my side, my cheek pressed to the cool floor.

*Mother, where are you?* I appealed from my thoughts- screaming my silent cry out into the world. I waited but received no answer.

Where was she? She had been searching for me for years and now that I wanted her to find me, she was nowhere to be found. I sighed as hot tears ran down my frigid cheeks. The dungeon was cold enough to hang meat in, strangely not cold enough to numb my pain.

And where was Brennan? I could only hope that Mormo hadn't caught up with him but Brennan almost had no chance. He had only just now discovered his abilities. There was no way he could withstand an attack by Mormo. Mormo was too ancient, too powerful. And I wasn't there to protect him. My heart ached with the thought.

His dreams. The thought occurred to me in an instant and I knew how I could reach him. But first I had to fall asleep… an impossible task. My thoughts were spinning too quickly for my body to relax enough for sleep.

Sleep.

Sleep.

*Sleep.* I commanded myself.

I consciously relaxed each muscle, working my way from my toes to my neck. The cold emanating from the floor didn't do much to help relax me, but I battled on. I had to sleep. As I went through the motions again, I focused on Brennan's handsome face, his sparkling grin. How had I let this happen? He was helpless now and it was my fault.

My fault.

Ugh. This wasn't helping. I flipped onto my other side and started the entire relaxation process again, trying to focus on Brennan's face without feeling the overwhelming guilt…a near-impossible task.

Once again, I focused on relaxing my toes, my legs, my abdomen. As I did, I envisioned each of those parts on Brennan's body. His toes as he had curled them over the side of the boat in the Aegean sea, his legs as he had balanced on the top of the Gryphon, his bare abdomen as he had held me in the haunted house.

My heart ached, but my body relaxed. And I fell asleep with Brennan in my mind. I re-emerged in his.

It was as bright as the sun, something I guess I should have expected. Golden light flooded his thoughts and I sought him out, desperate to see him safe and sound.

"Brennan?" I cried, the light here almost blinding.

"Empusa?" he asked in confusion, emerging from water. I recognized it immediately. He had been dreaming of the Sea of Tranquility. I gulped.

"Are you getting your peace on?" I tried to act casual, but gave up and flew into his strong arms. He closed them around me, holding me tightly against his hard chest.

"Where are you?" I cried against him, as my tears soaked us both. "Mormo's trying to find you. You're not safe."

"*I'm* not safe?" he pulled away slightly, his bronze eyebrow raised. "*You're* not safe, princess. I'm trying to find your mother. Don't worry about me. You taught me a few things. I'll be fine."

I laid my head against him again. "I didn't teach you enough," I fretted, my fingers clutching the strong muscles of his back.

"You taught me plenty," he assured me as he stroked my shoulder. "And I'm not an imbecile. I'll be fine. I'm figuring a few things out on my own. I'm going to find your mother and we will save you. I promise you that."

I looked up at him with watery eyes.

"I don't think so," I admitted. "I don't think it's possible. I either have to stay here with Poseidon or he will hand me over to Mormo and you know that my father will kill me. I don't think I'm going to come out of this. But I want you to be safe. Get far, far away from here. Promise me that."

He stared down at me, his hazel eyes turning butterscotch.

"Brennan, promise me, "I pleaded. "I can't stand the thought of something happening to you. Especially since it will be my fault. None of this would have happened if it weren't for me."

He sighed heavily and pulled me against him once again. "If I hadn't met you, my soul wouldn't have been awakened, Empusa. I feel like you kissed it – and woke it from a long slumber—something fairy tales are made of."

I glared at him. "Fairy tales have happy endings, Brennan."

"And we will have ours," he assured me, his tone confident. "I promise you, Emmie."

The familiarity of the new nickname made me gulp hard before I spoke.

"You should never promise something that you can't deliver," I told him. "This is impossible, Brennan. There's no way. Please, promise me that you will get away from here."

"I always deliver, Empusa," Brennan told me seriously, his handsome face confident. "I promise you that." He bent down to kiss my lips, his as soft and gentle as honey. I sighed and as I did, I woke up.

And I realized with a start that I wasn't alone.

"Hello, Empusa," a quiet voice said from the corner. With a gasp, I recognized the voice at once. The husky, confident, sexiness that emanated from the sound was unmistakable.

The god of the Underworld himself.

Hades.

# Chapter Fourteen

"What are you doing here?" I gasped as I flipped into a defensive crouch and eyed him cautiously. Hades laughed smoothly, completely unconcerned.

"Ah, little Empusa," Hades drawled, remaining completely motionless a few steps away from me. I realized that he was purposely trying to seem un-threatening. I relaxed only a slight bit. He laughed again, a throaty, sexy sound. I swallowed. Something about him caused a knot to clench in my stomach.

Hades tossed his shoulder-length glossy dark hair out of his eyes and I realized that he was every bit as handsome as a rock star and that's exactly the kind of feel that he exuded. Sexy, understated, charismatic. He was handsome without trying, magnetic without effort. I was drawn to him even though I didn't want to be. I swallowed again.

"I'm not here to hurt you, little Empusa," he assured me again. "Truly. You can trust me."

"Trust the god of the Underworld?" I raised my eyebrow incredulously. "Ha! That's a joke. You imprisoned me once already at the whim of my father. Why would I trust you again?"

Hades looked around us at the stark stone walls of my prison and raised a perfectly sculpted dark eyebrow.

"Have you a choice?" he asked quietly. "I don't see that you do. If you stay here, Poseidon will force you to his will. I doubt you will enjoy being raped. And if he turns you over to Mormo, well, that's a fate worse than death."

"Worse than death?" I was incredulous.

"Of course, young one," Hades answered. "Do you not know… you are an immortal. Mormo cannot kill you himself. Only Zeus' sword can do that heinous deed. But there are fates worse than death. Mormo could trap you in the wastelands. You would wish every minute that you could simply die. Is that what you want?"

"Of course not. My mother secured my freedom from you," I began haltingly. Hades held up his hand.

"Harmonia secured your freedom," he corrected politely. "Your mother arranged for us to meet so that I could remove your curse. But you never came. Why is that?"

Hades moved behind me quicker than I could even register, resting his warm hands on my shoulders as he leaned in next to my ear. His touch was feather light, like cashmere or air.

"You weren't afraid of me, were you?" he breathed softly, his lips a mere breadth from my cheek. If I wished, I could lean into him, into that husky voice. I mentally shook myself. What the hell? I didn't want him. Yet something about Hades made me think that I did.

"What is it about you?" I asked. "What draws me to you so much?"

He shrugged. "It's a gift. Or a curse. Just something about me, I guess." He shrugged again.

As he did, it occurred to me. Of course- his magnetism was one of his abilities. If he was unbearably charismatic, he could lure anyone he wanted into the Underworld. It was perfectly clear now.

"You're a bright one, *Emmie*," he drawled, pulling away slightly. I yanked away from him.

"Don't call me that!" I snapped. He looked at me innocently.

"Why ever not?" he held out his hands helplessly and then his voice hardened. "Because that's what your boyfriend, the son of Apollo, calls you?"

"How did you..." I trailed off.

Hades was the god of the Underworld. For all I knew, he could rifle through all of my thoughts if he wished. As soon as I thought it, the corners of his mouth curved slightly and I decided it must be the truth. He could hunt through my mind for any information that he wished.

And that was dangerous.

Everything about Hades was dangerous. His impossible magnetism, his cunning, his potential ruthlessness, his charm. He was very, very dangerous.

"Oh, not so much as you would notice," he answered my thought glibly and I cringed on the inside. I would need to focus on blocking my thoughts from him. The only way to protect myself from him was to protect the innermost workings of my mind. Hades flew once more to my side.

"It won't help," he murmured conspiratorially. "Everyone always thinks that they can secure their thoughts from me. What they don't realize is that it's impossible. I can find anything inside your mind that I need. It's just another gift."

He ran his hands up and down my arms soothingly and by the gods, I actually did find it soothing. I wanted to yank away- far away from him- but at the same time, I wanted to stay. I wanted to step inside his embrace and never leave it. That thought was petrifying.

"Please don't," I pleaded softly. "I don't want to feel this way."

"No?" One dark eyebrow arched gracefully above a dark brown eye.

"No." I was firm.

He sighed. "Well, more's the pity. But that doesn't affect my purpose here. You need to come with me. Now. If you do not, you are sealing your fate to a life worse than death. What do you choose?"

He held out his hand, long and graceful, and I watched it suspended in midair. His fingers curled just slightly, his fingernails perfectly manicured. It was something that didn't surprise me.  This was not a man who would own a callous.  Gritting my teeth, I stretched out my own hand and grasped his elegant fingers.

Instantly, we were gone.

\* \* \*

We emerged in a darkened sitting room where a fire roared in a massive stone fireplace across the room. Beautiful, expensive paintings adorned the walls and magnificent woven rugs were beneath my feet.  It smelled like roasted nuts and vanilla, a musky oriental scent.

"Welcome to my home," Hades bowed and released my hand.

"Empusa?" a voice called out, echoing through the large, warm room.  I looked around quickly, only to find someone flying out of one of the wing-backed chairs toward me.  I backed away out of reflex until I recognized the stream of blonde hair.

My mother.

I gasped and stilled.

"Mother?" My voice was barely above a whisper, my heart very quiet in my chest.  How could this be?

"Empusa!" she hurled into me with all the strength of a locomotive and I went flying backward. We landed in a flurry of arms and legs on the ground. My mother pulled away to look at me.

"It's really you? You're truly alright?"

Her voice was anxious and motherly, causing relief to flood through me. But she was here in the Underworld. I didn't understand that.

"Mother, why are you here?" I asked as I uncurled myself from her grasp and crawled to my feet. She looked at me in confusion.

"Empusa, why wouldn't I be? I've been trying to get you here for a long time."

I looked from her to Hades and back to her. Suddenly, comprehension dawned on me, draining the blood from my face.

"You arranged this?" I whispered again. Judging by her expression of guilt, I knew I was right. "You tricked me. You somehow arranged everything with Poseidon to get me here, didn't you?"

She was still and her cheeks pale as she registered the anger in my voice.

"Empusa, you don't understand. You never understood the danger that you were in. You needed to come here. You had no idea how important it was."

"So you arranged it. I want you to say the words. You tricked me, mother."

She nodded curtly. "For your own good, I arranged it, yes."

"And what of Brennan?" I asked haltingly. Hades had faded from my attention by this point. My eyes were focused on my mother. She was almost apologetic when she answered.

"You cannot be with Brennan," she finally said, true regret washing across her lovely features. "I'm so sorry, Empusa. But you cannot. The magic... the power that you would create together would be too much, impossible to control. It is for your own good that you stay away from him."

I shook my head, trying to make everything make sense. "So, how did you do it? I know you weren't working with Mormo. What did you do?"

"I teamed with Poseidon, of course," she shrugged. "At my behest, he reached out to Mormo, making the offer: your Moonstone for your life. All Mormo had to do was deliver you to Poseidon and Poseidon agreed to turn his back when Mormo stole you away."

"But Poseidon didn't mean it, right? So what will happen when Mormo discovers the truth? He's searching for Brennan right now, you know. What if he finds him before I do?"

"Empusa," my mother's voice was stern. "You are not going after that boy. I will make certain that Mormo never finds him. It will be impossible anyway. Hades is going to bring Mormo back here and imprison him in the Underworld forever. Mormo will never be a threat to you again."

I looked to Hades, who at this point was almost a shadow on the edge of the room. "Is that true?" I asked him. "Are you going to undo my curse and put it back on its rightful owner… finally?"

I was afraid to hope, my breath caught in my throat. My fingers shook as I waited for him to speak. And he took his time. His dark eyes appraised me, taking everything about me in as if he was drinking in the details. His gaze swept from my head to my feet and back again. And finally, when I thought I would die from suspense, he nodded.

"Of course, I am certainly willing to uphold my end of the bargain. With one small caveat."

My head snapped up at the same time as my mother's.

"Hades," she cautioned warningly, her voice dangerously calm. "There is no turning back. You gave your word."

Hades returned her gaze without flinching, seemingly unafraid. Most were afraid of my mother. To not fear her was either stupid or very, very brave.

"Hecate," he answered smoothly. "You created a bracelet enchanted with power that could be used over some in my realm. Any creature of the night can be affected by the spells that you used, controlled against their will. And when my subjects are affected, that is my concern. When you destroy that bracelet, I will destroy the curse. Fair is fair."

I hated to admit it, but he was right. If anyone who fell under the moon's realm could be controlled by my bracelet in the same way that Poseidon had controlled me, that wasn't right. And the bracelet should be destroyed.

"Mother, he's right," I turned to her. "Poseidon had quite the fun time showing me that he could control me with that thing. It isn't right to allow it to remain in the world if it could be used against someone else."

"Empusa," my mother's voice was pained and thin, something that startled me. She was always collected, always calm. If she showed emotion, something was wrong.

"What?" my voice was a whisper.

"You don't understand," she replied weakly. "I did what I had to do to protect you from your father. You don't understand how much he is capable of. I did what I had to do…"

Her voice trailed off and I struggled to breathe.

"What did you do?" I asked stiltedly. My breath felt like it was coming in short pants and each one was harder than the one before it.

Her cornflower eyes stared into mine and the pain I found there was striking, taking my limited breaths away.

"What?" I breathed.

My mother squared her shoulders. "You are tied to the Moonstone," she stated simply. "If it is destroyed, so too shall you be. It was the only way. I had to ensure your protection. If Mormo had ever managed to steal you, I would have been able to find you with the Moonstone. It's why I did it, why I took the risk. It was worth it to keep you safe." She dropped her hands limply.

"And am I safe now?" I asked quietly. She looked away and shook her head.

"You knew this, yet you allow Poseidon to hold it?" The anger in my voice was causing it to shake, even though I tried to maintain my control. It was a feat that got more difficult by the moment.

"It was the only way," she offered sadly. "I'm on my way right not to retrieve it from him. Empusa, the risks were worth your safety."

"Mother, you do not know Poseidon as well as you think you do if you believe that he will simply hand it over to you. He finally has something that no one else has ever had but the Fates themselves: leverage over you, the goddess of witchcraft. Don't think that he won't use it to his best advantage."

My mother looked miserable.

"He would not dare cross me," she announced fiercely. "I would make his life a living hell. And I am not an idiot, Empusa. There is but one thing that can destroy the Moonstone- Zeus' sword. In which case, one would have to appeal to Zeus and ask him to destroy it. It wouldn't happen without good reason. Trust me, he would not do such a thing for Poseidon."

I felt an ounce of relief. Zeus would likely require a very good reason for using his sword to destroy it. My life was probably safe- for now. But the thought that my life was tied to a trinket, a bracelet that had dangled carelessly on my wrist for years… it was unsettling.

"Mother, you should have told me," I admonished seriously. "I never had any idea of the importance of that stone."

"I know," she answered sadly. "There was never a good time. I told you to guard it with your life. I told you to never take it off."

"And I didn't," I answered. "Because I trusted you."

She took a step toward me and grabbed my hand. "Empusa, you're my daughter. I love you more than anything else in all the world. I would not jeopardize you for anything. You must trust that creating the Moonstone was the only way that I could guarantee your safety."

I yanked my hand away and took a few steps away from her.

"Mother, what do you not understand? It wasn't necessary. You thought I wouldn't be safe on my own, yet I've managed to elude you and stay safe for years. You've allowed who you are to cloud your judgment. You are not invincible and other people are competent besides you. I don't see why you can't understand that. What you have done in creating the Moonstone was not protect me but jeopardize me. You have put me at risk. *You*."

Her face crumbled with my words and I felt a fleeting sense of guilt, but tampered it down. This was something she needed to hear.

"Mother, I love you. But this is not right. And you need to fix it. I am going to trust you now. I am going to find Brennan. You need to put this to rights. Retrieve the Moonstone from Poseidon. Appeal to Zeus. See if there is any way that we can remove my connection with it in order to destroy it. If not, then I guess I'll have to remain cursed forever. But for now, see what you can do. If anyone can fix this, you can."

I glanced at Hades and my mother only once before I closed my eyes and faded from the Underworld. My mother's expression of pain lingered with me though and I knew that I would carry it with me forever.

# Chapter Fifteen

I burst into the mortal world as I hit the ground running on the empty fairways of AdventureLand. I wasn't sure what had made me come here. I just knew that if I was Brennan, this might be where I would stay. It was out of the way, no one else would think of it and it was the last place in the mortal world we had been together.

An early snowfall had carpeted the paved walkways in white flakes that glistened in the sun and I crunched through them as I ran toward the haunted house. A flock of blackbirds startled as I ran past and scattered screaming into the sky as I leapt lightly onto the porch.

Throwing the door wide open, I sprinted for the room that we had turned into our makeshift hide-out, bounding over the metal tracks and rubber hoses that littered my path. I almost didn't dare to hope, but even still… I had a feeling in the pit of my stomach. I couldn't explain it. I just felt as though he was here.

"Brennan!" I yelled as I skidded around the corner and into the bedroom.

Brennan stared at me in surprise from the middle of the bed amidst open books and stacks of maps. He was every bit as handsome as he was in my mind, his golden hair curling up at his collar, his hazel eyes widening in surprise as he registered who I was.

"Em," he breathed before he leapt from the bed, scattering his documents everywhere. He was by my side in one second flat. One beat later, I was clenched to his chest in a vice grip.

"What are you doing here?" he asked quickly before he crushed my lips with his own. "You're not safe here," he muttered against my lips before he kissed me frantically again. Then again. And again. His lips were like satin, his breath like honey. I found that I wanted to pour him into a glass and drink him and I tightened my arms around his muscled waist.

"You're not safe here, either," I told him with an ironic smile. I found it funny that he was concerned with my safety while there was a psychotic immortal chasing him. "I don't have my bracelet anymore, so truly, neither of us is safe."

"Is it bad that nothing else seems to matter as long as you're with me?" Brennan asked quietly as he inhaled my neck. I stretched out my chin to give him better access as I shook my head and grasped him tightly.

"No. It's not bad. It's exactly how I feel. I love you, Brennan. Don't ever leave me like that again or I swear by the gods that I will kill you myself."

I felt him smile against my skin, before he lightly kissed it.

"Well, that's romantic," he announced as he pulled away to look at me. "Empusa, I had to leave. I have to find your mother. You'll never be safe until I do."

Sighing, I grasped his hand. "Well, now, that's another story altogether."

At his confused look, I led him to the bed and sat with him, telling him everything that had transpired since he had left Poseidon's palace. When I was finished, he was left with his mouth hanging open. I reached over and gently closed it.

"Why are you so surprised?" I asked him wearily. "I've told you. In the world of the Olympians, nothing is ever what it seems. Not anything."

His jaw tightened. "Your mother meant well, I'm sure. But…"

I interrupted him. "I know. She has inadvertently put me at risk. I told her. And I have told her to fix it. And I have faith that she will."

"And in the meantime?"

I sighed. For the very first time in my life, I wasn't sure what to do.

"I don't know," I admitted.

Brennan raised an eyebrow. "No?"

"No."

"Well, I have an idea," he suggested, slipping one arm under my knees and scooping me to his chest.

I laid my forehead against the warmth that I found there and sighed with contentment. Perhaps I shouldn't be so happy to be here. I had brought nothing but danger to Brennan's life. But I couldn't deny it. There was no place else I'd rather be.

He sat on the edge of the bed and balanced me carefully on his legs. "Rest for a while, Emmie. You seem tired. You've been through a lot. You must be exhausted. Let me hold you while you sleep. I promise you, no one will get to you."

I hadn't realized how tired I actually was, how bone weary, until he pointed it out. But I was so tired that my legs were literally shaking. Even still, there were things we had to discuss. I resisted the urge to lean my head against him and close my eyes.

"Brennan, I don't think you understand. My mother said that it is too dangerous for us to be together, that we can never be together. If that is true, what will become of us? I can't stand the thought of being without you...but I can't bear the thought of any harm coming to you, either."

A tear slipped down my cheek and Brennan seemed bothered as he wiped it gently away with his thumb. His forehead was wrinkled in thought as he bent to gently kiss the spot where the tear had been.

"Emmie," he began softly and my heart contracted at his voice. The very sound of it set me ablaze. "I don't care what anyone says. You and I will find a way to be together. I don't care what it takes, how long it takes or what I have to do. You belong with me. Got it?"

I nodded silently, finally allowing my eyes to close as I breathed him in... his strength, his scent, everything. He was right. I belonged to him and he belonged to me. I almost pitied the person who tried to tear us apart because I would take them down limb by limb.

"You're a feisty little hellcat, aren't you?" he murmured as he read my mind. I smiled without opening my eyes.

"I keep forgetting you can do that now," I answered sleepily. "I've got to be careful. I don't want you to learn all of my secrets."

He laughed, a gentle, low sound in the dark.

"I already know your secrets," he replied confidently. "And I'm still here. So you see, I'm never going anywhere."

I snuggled closer into his arms and allowed the darkness to overtake me as Brennan settled into the pillows behind us. But my sleep was interrupted before it had even begun.

"Empusa," a calm voice said near my ear. I startled to attention and sat straight up.

Gaia stepped from the edge of the shadows and knelt by my side, her jewelry jingling as she moved. I sighed a breath of relief and Brennan grasped my arm.

"What is it?" he asked worriedly.

Gaia smirked. "He doesn't know you can see me?"

I glared at her. "It's not because I was keeping it from him. I just haven't had the opportunity to share that particular thing."

Brennan leaned forward and murmured into my ear. "Who are you talking to? Or do I not want to know?"

I met his gaze. "It depends. How do you feel about ghosts?"

He raised one blonde eyebrow. "Ghosts? Really?"

I nodded. "Definitely. One loud-mouthed ghost is perched on the edge of this bed. Her name is Gaia. She died in ancient Rome and she is one of my best friends in the world."

Brennan sighed patiently, his hazel eyes flickering toward Gaia's general vicinity. "And you know this how?"

"I'm over here, Romeo," Gaia announced, making a circular motion in front of her face. I glared at her.

"As if he can see you."

"And you can?" Brennan asked. He almost looked amused by this point, as though nothing surprised him anymore. I decided that was a healthy attitude for him to have and nodded.

"Yes. I can see her. I can see all ghosts, actually. It's an ability I have because of my mother. Ghosts fall under her realm."

"Ah, yes. The moon, witchcraft and all things dark?"

"Now you've got it," I commended him laughingly. "All things dark."

"And I come from all things light," he mused. "It's no wonder we're supposedly incompatible."

I shook my head. "Apparently it's not that we're incompatible. It's because our combined energy would be too much for us to control or something like that. It's hard to say if my mother was telling me the whole story."

Gaia interrupted. "How exactly would your energy 'combine', Empusa?" I glanced at her to find her concealing an ornery smile.

"You know exactly how," I mumbled. "We'd probably have to... well, we'd have to..."

"You'd have to have sex?" she chirped impishly, knowing full well that this topic made me uncomfortable, particularly with Brennan next to me. I swatted at Gaia, my hand swiping fruitlessly down through the air.

"Yes," I answered clearly and defiantly. "In order for our energy to combine, I think we'd have to have sex."

Brennan's head snapped to attention, his eyes twinkling.

"Really?" he asked hopefully. "Then perhaps we should test that theory out. There's no way to rule it out unless we perform an experiment. I'm up for it," he offered. "Just so you know."

I shook my head and rolled my eyes toward Gaia. "Mortals."

Brennan laughed, a sound so delicious that even Gaia paused to appreciate it. She cocked her head and studied him thoughtfully.

"He's sexy, Empusa," she declared. "I'll give you that. But I do think that you're mother might be right. There's a chemistry between the two of you. I can feel it in the air, even when you're sitting here doing nothing. If you did anything…er, *else,* I'm afraid Hecate might be right. Your energy would be too hard to contain."

"First, it's not polite to talk about someone when they can't hear you," I told her. "Second, it's very possible that we might have a problem outside of the bedroom as well. I think that as Brennan's powers further develop—that fact itself might cause a problem for us. Our powers might be contradictory or something. I only just now thought of that when you pointed out the electricity in the room right now. I feel it too and it's stronger now than it was before."

Brennan nodded seriously in agreement. "I feel it too."

"It would be impossible not to," Gaia grumbled. "It's practically making my hair stand on end." She needlessly smoothed her neat long hair as she spoke. "I think you might be right, Empusa."

The more I thought on it, the more convinced I was that I was right, as well. And it wasn't a comforting thought. I wanted Brennan to improve upon his abilities. I wanted him to master everything he was capable of. But at the same time, the thought terrified me now. The stronger he became, the more danger we posed to each other. How unfair was that?

Brennan read my mind. I could tell because he watched my face and as soon as my thoughts registered with him, his forehead wrinkled…a tell-tale sign of his concern.

"Crap," he muttered.

"Yikes! Crap is right!" Gaia exclaimed, digging in her cloak as though she'd forgotten something. I watched her curiously.

"What is it?"

She found what she was looking for and extended her hand to me. I opened mine and she dropped my Moonstone bracelet into my waiting palm. My eyes widened immediately as Brennan took a sharp breath behind me.

"What the hell? How…"

"Your mom sent me with it," Gaia answered proudly, obviously impressed that my mother trusted her enough for this sort of important mission. "I was supposed to give it only to you. She also sent this."

Gaia handed me a small rolled papyrus, tied with a soft crimson cord. I tugged the cord free and unrolled the missive. My mother's flowing hand spilled onto the page.

*I do hope that this is proof that you can trust me,*
*daughter. I love you more than life. Protect the moonstone*
*until we set everything to rights.*


I looked up at Gaia, my eyes wet with tears. "How did she get it back from Poseidon so quickly? Why didn't she bring it herself? And how did she know to give it to you?"

Gaia stared back at me. "Your mother knows far more than you give her credit for," she answered carefully. "She knew that you wouldn't want to see her right now, even though apparently she could have used the Moonstone to find you. It is what led me to you, as a matter-of-fact. And I don't know how she got it back from Poseidon. I think she had leverage of some sort."

"Well, obviously," I answered absently. "And knowing Poseidon's nature, I'm sure he's given her plenty of ammunition for leverage throughout the years."

"No doubt," Gaia agreed, her eyes glittering in the dark. "Now what, princess? Your mother has gone to the Spiritlands to discuss this situation with Zeus. You've got to keep yourself away from your father until everything is resolved and you've got to avoid internally combusting over this guy." She gestured toward Brennan.

"I'm not going to internally combust," I replied, reaching to grasp Brennan's hand. He rubbed his thumb in a circle over mine, a familiar, comforting gesture. "But we'll have to be careful. I just wish I had more information to go on. My whole situation is so strange. If only…" My voice trailed off as an idea popped into my head.

"What is it?" Brennan asked curiously. "What have you thought of?"

"Harmonia," I answered slowly. "She's the only one who even comes close to knowing what I feel like. She was cursed because of a stone- the Bloodstone. It ended up being because Zeus' blood was embedded within it, which eventually saved all of the Olympians from the Fates. But Harmonia didn't know that until everything was finished. That Bloodstone controlled her for thousands of years. I want to talk to her about it."

"But didn't you say that she lives in the Underworld?" Brennan asked hesitantly. "We're not dead. How would we go about getting there?"

"You could do it the old fashioned way," Gaia suggested with a shrug.

"You mean the *dead* way," I clarified. Gaia smiled as she nodded.

"It's not so bad," she answered. "You'd never age."

"I never age as it is," I replied wryly. "I'll think we'll go in another direction. Hades took me with him awhile ago. We went straight to the Underworld. We were able to bypass the ferryman, the gates, the Judgment room, everything. I'll just summon Hades."

I shrugged like it was no big deal, like interacting with the god of the Underworld was a normal, everyday thing. Like he didn't want to keep my soul in the Underworld with him forever, like he wasn't sexy as hell and almost impossible to resist.

I sighed. If you were going to live, you might as well live dangerously.

# Chapter Sixteen

"I knew you'd come to me sooner or later, little kitten," Hades purred smoothly. He stood proudly in my dream, looking exactly like a rock star. He wore an unbuttoned white silk that flowed around his wrists, black leather pants and a black cloak that seemed to swirl around him even though there was no breeze.

"Don't misinterpret," I warned him, circling him cautiously.

Even while I was dream-walking, I didn't want to turn my back to him. It just didn't seem wise. He smiled as he realized what I was doing. His teeth were brilliantly white in contrast to his olive skin.

"I simply need access to the Underworld. I'm not here for you."

"You certainly know how to sweet talk someone," Hades replied glibly, before his handsome features hardened slightly. "Why should I help you? What could I possibly have to gain?"

"Mormo," I uttered softly, watching Hades face. "Mormo has eluded you for years. How do you think that looks to the outside world? The god of the Underworld has been outmaneuvered."

Hades' face clouded over for a scant second before he recovered and I felt a small bit of satisfaction. It had been a calculated gamble, but I had been right. It did bother Hades that Mormo had always been one step ahead of him.

"Do you think that I haven't allowed Mormo's freedom?" Hades asked smoothly. "At any given time, I could have located him and brought him to me in manacles and chains. But I did not. Why? Because *you* have never upheld your side of the bargain and appeared in front of me."

"Why should I have had to?" I asked gently. "I never did anything wrong. Mormo is the one who sacrificed me. I never gave my permission."

"I didn't need your permission," Hades replied grittily, although a fleeting expression of something... remorse?... passed over his face. "I'm the god of the Underworld and I do what is best for my kingdom. I'm sorry, little Empusa, but you would have been better for my kingdom than Mormo's black soul."

"But that's neither here nor there," I answered thickly, trying not to allow emotions to well up and make me cry. "You gave your word in front of every Olympian. You have to uphold it now."

Hades shook his head impatiently. "We've been through this. I am perfectly willing to do so, but there is that tiny complication with your Moonstone and your life. I assume you want to live so the Moonstone cannot be destroyed and that is my one condition for reversing Mormo's curse. I'm sorry, Empusa. Surely you can understand my position. We're at a stalemate."

"I'm not here to beg you for leniency," I snapped. "I'm not here to discuss that situation at all, actually. I'm here to ask for your help."

He looked amused.

"My help? Pray tell, how can I be of service to you?" he asked sardonically and I saw a brief glimpse of impatience. He masked it quickly, though. He was very accustomed to being charming and smooth no matter the circumstance.

"I need to enter your kingdom," I said simply. "I only wish to speak to Harmonia and since she cannot leave but to visit her parents in the Spiritlands, I wish to go to her."

"And you don't wish to meet her in the Spiritlands. Hmm. I wonder why? Could it be that you do not trust my brother, Zeus?" Hades pondered, his brow wrinkled just slightly as he thought. "It is wise to tread lightly around him," he added in approval. "I can understand why you don't wish to travel there."

"It's not that I don't trust Zeus, per se," I replied carefully. "It is just that I know that my existence is a small thing to him. I'm not sure if he still holds a grudge against my mother for helping the Fates… and you…

and I don't wish to appear in front of him until I hear that all is well on that front."

"That is fairly wise, little kitten," Hades answered approvingly. "Fine. I will help you. I'll accompany you to the Underworld so that you can meet with Harmonia. What is it that you wish to see her about, anyway?"

"That's not really your concern, is it?" I snapped, then thought the better of it. "I mean, she and I went through a similar trauma. I was trapped in the Underworld and so was her daughter. I'd like to discuss it with her."

Hades stared at me thoughtfully and I knew that he was rifling through my thoughts. I tried my best to block them, simply because I didn't like the idea that he was in my head. His lips twitched as he read that thought, but he concealed his smile.

"Alright, Empusa," he said softly, placing his hand on my shoulder. His touch was appealing, but I ignored it as best I could. "We'll do it your way. I don't really need to know your purpose in seeing Harmonia. It's of little consequence to me."

I knew that was a lie, but I didn't say it. Instead, I simply nodded.

"Thank you," I murmured. "I'll need to take Brennan as well."

Hades met my gaze, his dark eyes smoldering. Why did he have to be so breathtakingly sexy?

"Very well," he nodded. "The son of Apollo is welcome in my home. For now. Wake, little Empusa and we shall go."

My eyes fluttered open.

I was safely ensconced within Brennan's strong arms, but there was a difference in the air and my gaze flew around the room. Hades stood in the corner, waiting for me to wake.

I felt Brennan's sharp intake of breath as chest expanded against my back. He tightened his grip and I knew that he innately knew who was lurking in our room.

"I think introductions are in order," Brennan said smoothly, strong and assured. I was proud of him, at his restraint, his assurance. It was one of the things that I loved about him. He was so confident and self-assured.

Hades stepped casually from the shadows and I noted that Gaia was nowhere to be found. I was certain that at the first sign of Hades, she had fled. She had no desire to be carted to the Underworld.

"Oh, I think you know who I am, son of Apollo," Hades drawled as he strolled to our bedside and stared down at us. Since we were only napping, we were fully clothed and I was suddenly thankful for it.

"And I think you're aware of my name," Brennan answered firmly. "You should use it."

Hades appraised him slowly and I realized that I was holding my breath. He was the King of the Underworld, after all. He was no more to be trifled with than Zeus or Poseidon. Apparently, he took no offense, though, and his shoulders relaxed.

"You're pleasing to me, son of Apollo," Hades answered with a smile. "You have the beauty of your father, but you are much smarter. I like your energy. Perhaps you would be able to convince Empusa to dwell in my world. I think you and she would be very happy there and you would make positive additions to the Underworld. You should think on it."

Brennan stared back at him, his gaze shifting from hazel to butterscotch. "I'll accompany Empusa wherever she wishes to go," he answered calmly. "Whether it is to the Spiritlands, the Underworld or the mortal world. If she is there, then I am happy."

"How very diplomatic of you," Hades answered. "I personally tell Persephone what I will be doing and she adjusts her thinking accordingly. You should try it sometime."

I couldn't help but laugh at that. Hades might stray from his wife from time to time, but he definitely loved her to distraction. His love for her was well known and even documented in mortal mythology books. He glanced at me, but didn't say anything about my amusement.

"Are you ready to go?" he asked stoutly, glossing over it.

"Whenever you are," I answered, getting up and pulling Brennan to his feet.

"Very well then," Hades answered. "Let us be gone."

And we were.

* * *

We appeared on the porch of a replica of Zeus' palace, which sat on a replica Mount Olympus. Everything surrounding us was replicated from the actual Mount Olympus down to the smallest detail. It was how Hades and the Fates had tricked the Olympians into eating here... which is how they had imprisoned them here for several millennia. It was a law in the world of the immortals: Anyone who eats in the Underworld must stay in the Underworld. It was also how Hades had managed to keep Persephone here.

"This is incredible," Brennan breathed as he stared around us in fascination.

"Yes," I agreed. "But whatever you do, do not eat anything here."

Hades glanced at me sardonically and I smiled pleasantly back at him in return. And I understood Brennan's amazement. The Isles of the Blessed were even more beautiful than Atlantis, a feat that one would think impossible unless they were standing right here.

"This is unreal," Brennan added as he pivoted on the porch to take in all of the scenery.

Lush, tropical breezes caressed our faces and fruity, delicious scents filled the air. The smells of peaches, mangoes and apricots blended with the salt from the sea to create a magnificent, unique smell. It was something you would only find here. The Isles of the Blessed were truly a paradise.

Greenery lined elegant, sculpted pathways while brightly colored birds sat on the limbs of healthy, swaying trees nearby. Elegant flowers tossed their fragrances into the wind and large blue Lotus blossoms drifted down from the air landing softly on the ground. Brennan made a motion to bend towards one and I grabbed his arm.

"Don't," I reminded him. "They are delicious, but eating will imprison you here. You can try the Lotus blossoms in the real Spiritlands."

"If you're ever brave enough to take him there, little kitten," Hades purred from beside me. I glared at him but didn't have time to retort because the heavy doors of the palace were thrown open and a little girl faced us.

"Em!" she cried happily before throwing herself into my arms.

"Raquel," I murmured into her dark hair. Her skinny little arms clutched at my neck and I lifted her easily to hold her. "How have you been, little one?"

"I love it here, Em!" she told me happily. "I have a pet bird and I'm teaching him to talk. I can have anything I wish as long as mama and daddy say it is okay. Isn't that wonderful?"

She stared at me excitedly and I couldn't help but marvel once again at how much she looked like her mother. Both she and Harmonia had exquisite jade green eyes, so vivid that they seemed almost fake. She had glowing, healthy skin, dark hair that fell in glossy waves to the middle of her back and a bright, white smile. She didn't look dead, but she most certainly was.

Raquel had been one of the machinations of the Fates...just one of the many ways that they had tormented Harmonia. Harmonia had lived for a couple of thousand years thinking that she was a Keeper of Fate and that she worked for the three ancient sisters. They guided her into making horrendously difficult decisions-both for herself and her mother. In another cruel twist, her memories were taken by them. She didn't know who her mother truly was or even who she herself really was. It was rectified now, but it had wreaked havoc with her for years.

But Raquel had been affected by the aftermath of the Fates' deceit. Her very existence had been undone and she had been sent here, which is one of the reasons Harmonia had chosen to stay here. Her act had freed me to leave. At that particular moment, only one of us would have been able to go. I was in Harmonia's debt.

"Mama's going to be so happy," Raquel told me excitedly. "She's been wondering about you. But I don't know your friends," she added as she glanced at Hades and Brennan. She didn't seem concerned, she simply tugged on my hand. "Come on, Em. Let's go find her."

I fell into step with the little girl and we quickly wound our way through the opulent halls of the palace with Hades and Brennan right behind us. I couldn't see

Brennan's face as we navigated through the lavish palace, but I could feel his wonderment just as clearly as if he had spoken it aloud. This amazing place would be hard for any mortal to absorb.

As we pushed through a set of ornately carved ivory doors, I caught a glimpse of Harmonia and her husband, Cadmus, seated on a nearby patio outdoors. The breeze caught Harmonia's dark hair and Cadmus leaned over to laughingly tuck it behind her ear. Their loving familiarity had always caused me to ache deep inside, simply because I wanted what they had: a love that withstood the test of time.

However, today my heart did not ache. A quick glance toward Brennan reminded me why. I had someone to share my life with now, something that might withstand time just as well as Cadmus and Harmonia had. At my thought, Brennan caught my gaze and his impish grin caused my heart to skip a beat.

He reached over and brushed my hand with his own. "We can withstand anything," he assured me quietly. "Including time itself."

A knot formed in my throat and I struggled to swallow it as I nodded. He leaned over and brushed a kiss against my forehead.

"I mean that," he added thoughtfully. "Anything."

Hades snorted behind us but I didn't think twice about him. I was lost in the intensity of Brennan's stare. He truly meant what he said. I knew it with every ounce of my being. And it was a really good feeling. I hadn't trusted someone in such a way for a very long time.

"Mama!" Raquel cried, bringing me back to the matter at hand. Harmonia and Cadmus both turned their attention toward us. Harmonia's green eyes lit up as soon as she registered who I was.

"Empusa," she breathed, leaping up from her chair and blurring into motion to reach me. I had no sooner braced myself before she plowed into me, enclosing me in a grip that defied her slight stature.

"Where have you been?" Harmonia exclaimed, stroking my hair in a motherly fashion. "We've been looking all over for you!"

I wiggled away just slightly, giving myself enough room to breathe.

"I know and I'm really sorry," I told her sincerely. "I didn't mean to cause anyone worry. I was just afraid."

"I know," Harmonia interrupted kindly. "I'm not blaming you. We've just been so worried. It is a true blessing to set eyes upon you. That's all."

Her face was alight with relief and joy and it warmed my heart. There truly were good people out there in the world, mixed in with those who were evil. I had spent so long trying to elude my father that I sometimes lost sight of that.

"Thank you," I told her quickly. "For your kindness."

"My kindness?" she asked me with a raised eyebrow. "Empusa, you risked a great deal to keep my daughter safe. I'll never forget what you did and I'll never be able to repay you."

I grew uncomfortable with her glowing accolades. "Harmonia, you've already repaid me ten-fold. You stayed here so that I could leave. That was an unbelievable sacrifice. I'm the one who will never be able to repay *you*."

"Pssh," she dismissed my words with a shake of her head. "Let's simply agree to disagree. What brings you here to me today? Have you spoken with your mother?"

As Harmonia spoke, she rubbed my arm with her slender hands and her eyes finally drifted away from me. As her gaze passed over Hades, her eyes narrowed, but she didn't say anything. She was too intent with staring at Brennan.

"The son of Apollo," she murmured, a look of intense curiosity on her exquisite face. "Why have you brought the son of Apollo?"

Brennan looked at her with an expression of curiosity, humor and resignation. It seemed he'd grown accustomed to being called the son of Apollo. He stuck out his hand.

"I'm Brennan," he told her good-naturedly. "Apparently, I'm the son of Apollo."

Harmonia smiled and shook his hand, her Bloodstone pendant flashing crimson as it swung forward when she moved. Without thinking, I reached out and touched it, the glistening blood-red color pulling me in.

I immediately wished I hadn't. An intense bright light exploded behind my eyelids and brought me to my knees with its sheer force. Shooting pain radiated from my temples and I clutched my head. Images shot in and out of my mind in rapid succession, coming and going so quickly that I could barely register what they were before they were gone.

It was the future. And it wasn't pleasant.

# Chapter Seventeen

"Empusa, I'm so sorry," Harmonia apologized for the one-thousandth-time, as she sat next to me and brushed the hair away from my face. "I shouldn't have been so careless with my Bloodstone. It is known to illicit strong visions and emotions to those who touch it. I'm sorry that I didn't shield you from that."

Her perfect face was troubled and I hurried to reassure her, even though I still felt shaky and weak in the knees from what I had just seen.

"Harmonia, it wasn't your fault. But tell me, what *was that?*"

I grew increasingly cognizant enough to notice my surroundings and realized that Brennan sat to my side and that I was reclining on a plush lounge on the veranda. Harmonia, Hades, Raquel and Cadmus surrounded us and I took a deep, steadying breath.

*I am strong.*

*I am strong.*

*I am strong.*

I repeated the phrase to myself silently over and over, trying to remind myself. I could withstand anything. Nothing could faze me. I was strong.

"That's true," Brennan agreed with my silent thoughts. "You are very strong. But something just happened. What was it, Em?"

"I don't know," I replied softly. "I think I saw the future."

"The future?" Cadmus interjected, his bronzed face thoughtful. "That would be new. Usually, the Bloodstone grants visions of the past. What do you think, my love?" he asked Harmonia, stroking her shoulder lightly.

I could see that he was trying to hide something. Concern? But just as quickly as the emotion crossed his face, he reigned it in and replaced it with a calm, impassive expression.

"What exactly did you see, Empusa?" Harmonia asked calmly. Raquel sat at my feet and watched me worriedly. I tried to keep my expression calm and steady for her benefit, but it wasn't easy.

"Raquel," I focused on the nervous little girl. "Could you possibly run and get me some nectar? I'm dying for a drink."

"Of course, Empusa. I'll be right back," Raquel jumped from the lounge and took off for what I presumed was the kitchen. As soon as she was out of earshot, I refocused on the adults surrounding me.

"I think I saw the end of the world," I mumbled anxiously. I couldn't help it. My unease bled into my voice. My heart was racing and I couldn't calm down. The terrifying, scattered images had burned into my head and I couldn't get them out. Fire, floods, pain and tears. So many images crowded into my head and I struggled to block them out.

Harmonia stared into my eyes as she read my mind and tried to see what I had already seen. As she saw the images in my head, her vibrant green eyes widened then narrowed as she came to the same conclusion.

"It does seem like an apocalypse of some sort," she concurred, her thin shoulders slumping slightly. Cadmus stepped protectively up behind her, as if to guard her from an unseen threat. "But the question is... why?"

Brennan stared at me, troubled and pensive. "Yes, Em. Why?"

But I could see on his face that he already knew. He had seen it in my thoughts.

"My mother was right," I said simply, my breathing ragged in my throat, each breath more jagged than the last. "Together, Brennan and I are dangerous."

Brennan's forehead wrinkled and he grasped my hand. "Em, I don't accept that. We'll figure it out. It will be alright." But his voice was unsure, his gaze wavering. Like me, he desperately wanted it to be alright. But he had seen what I had.

"Brennan," my voice cracked and Harmonia looked away discreetly as a single tear slid hotly down my cheek. "There was so much blood. Oceans of it. People were screaming and crying...there was so much death and ugliness. We can't jeopardize the entire mortal world just because we want to be together. That would be irresponsible and cold-hearted. Neither of us is that."

I beseeched him pleadingly, hoping that he could offer an alternative, anything that would allow us to stay together. And I could see him thinking. I could hear his silent, desperate thoughts. But none of us, not a one, could come up with a viable option. I sighed as my heart constricted. I didn't want to live without Brennan. Even now, it seemed as though he had always been with me. He was a physical part of my soul. The idea of never seeing his brilliant smile again made me cringe.

He stroked my hand, his fingers strong. "It's not going to happen," he assured me. "We will be together. I'll think of something."

"Your bond is very strong," Harmonia nodded. "I can feel it. If you could think of some way to harness the positive energy of your bond instead of allowing your conflicting powers to explode around you, it could work, I think."

"It's a possibility," Cadmus agreed, his glossy black hair glistening in the light as he nodded toward his wife. "But it is something you will have to work at. It certainly won't be an easy task."

"We don't need easy," I stated tiredly. "We just need possible."

"Well, then, it sounds like we're golden because it's possible," Brennan gently smiled at me. "Emmie, I promise. I'll do whatever I have to do. I'll practice my abilities 24 hours a day. I'll stand on any roller coaster in the country for hours at a time. I'll do anything you tell me that we need to do. Just say the word."

"I don't know what word to say," I reminded him softly. "This is just a theory. We might be able to harness our bond to overcome our negative combined energy. Or we might not. It's just a theory. We have no idea how to put it into practice. That's a problem. Harmonia, do you have any ideas?"

"What about Hecate?" Raquel asked innocently, her eyes dewy and wide, standing on the edge of the room clutching a glass of nectar. I hadn't even heard her come back in. "Hecate helped my mama. Couldn't she help you, Empusa?"

I shook my head slightly. "I'm afraid not, Raquel. My mother is already trying to help. She's talking to Zeus on my behalf. I'm going to have to work this out on my own." I could hear the dejection in my own voice and that annoyed me. I squared my shoulders.

"Em," Harmonia said uncertainly. "What about your mother's cronies, Circes and Medea? Do you trust them to help? They certainly have proven loyal to your mother over the years."

I thought of the ancient hags, of their wrinkled wise faces, and I had to admit that it was a possibility. They knew more about magic than anyone on the planet besides my mother. And since my mother wasn't available, it was worth a try. If there was an answer to be found and if they were willing, they would be the ones to ask.

"That's actually a good idea," I told her with a smile. "It could work. They might know something."

"I'm not sure that you should attempt anything in the mortal world," Cadmus interrupted wisely. "You might want to contain your magic here in the Underworld. It would provide a buffer to the mortals while you practice."

His eyes clouded over as he recalled my visions of destruction... of all that could possibly happen to the mortal world if Brennan and I failed. Cadmus turned to me as he noticed that I was watching him worry.

"Do not fear," he assured me. "You can do this. There was a time when Harmonia turned the mortal world black with her sheer will. It was for a noble purpose and she prevailed. I have no qualms that you can do the same, little one. You can prevent harming the mortal world and still have personal happiness. There is a strength in you that few others have. I can see it."

"My husband is right," Harmonia agreed. "You have a backbone of steel, Em. I've never seen anything like it. If anyone can do this, you can. But we need to figure out the logistics. We have to protect the mortal world from your energy until you learn to control it. But we still need to get you to Circes and Medea." Her brow furrowed as she sought a solution.

"There's a secret portal," Raquel suggested in her girlish, songlike voice. We all turned to her in surprise.

"What secret portal?" Harmonia asked her quickly. "I don't know what you speak of, sweetling."

Raquel sighed patiently. "I found it when I was waiting for you here. There is a portal that the Fates created a long time ago. I think I can remember how to get to it. Anyone can enter from the mortal world but only the true of heart can use it to leave here." She turned to me. "And that won't be a problem for you, Em. You have the truest of hearts."

She patted my hand with her smaller one, much like a mother patting a child.

"But I don't want to leave here," I reminded her gently. "I want to get Circes and Medea in. I don't know if their hearts would be pure enough to leave." I sighed. They were ancient and throughout the ages, they had done some truly atrocious things.

"I might be persuaded to allow them to leave," Hades broke in, his voice as smooth as warm caramel. "You've piqued my curiosity now with this talk of an apocalypse. I can't decide… would the end of the mortal world be good or bad for the Underworld? I'm not certain. An apocalypse might ensure that I receive all mortal souls—but it would be at once. I might prefer to keep them straggling in over time as it currently stands. Until I decide, you may proceed with your plan. I will allow the hags to leave."

I had actually forgotten that Hades was even here. He had retreated to the outer edge of the room and had remained quiet as he observed us. He watched me now with a dark, unreadable expression on his outrageously handsome face. He was pensively reflective, a mood that disturbed me. It meant that his thoughts were churning which was something that might not bode well for the rest of us.

"Why would you help us?" I asked him curiously, my words mirroring Brennan's uncertain thoughts. Brennan's gaze met mine knowingly. He thought the same as I did, that Hades had an underlying motive.

"Yes, Hades," Harmonia added sharply. "What is in it for you? And do not tell me nothing. I know you better than that."

Hades' dark gaze smoldered for a scant second across the room before he blurred into motion toward Harmonia. He reached her before I even drew another breath, standing behind her with his mouth so close to her ear that he was almost touching her.

"Sweet Harmonia," he breathed quietly into her ear. "You do know me...better than so many people. Why must you always believe the worst of me?"

His teeth glinted white against his olive skin and I found myself leaning toward him unconsciously. I caught myself and moved back, just as Cadmus lunged toward him. In one deft move, Cadmus lifted the god of the Underworld and hurled him into the far wall.

There was a collective gasp as Hades smashed into the wall of priceless vases, sending shattered glass skittered across the gleaming floor. He rolled to his feet and faced Cadmus in a defensive stance.

"Choose your actions carefully, soldier," Hades instructed smoothly, seemingly unruffled. His lip was bleeding though, tangible evidence that he had been injured. Everything else about him seemed smooth and undisturbed. "Watch yourself."

"Keep your hands off of my wife," Cadmus growled. "You have no right to touch her. Watch *yourself.*"

"My, my, Cadmus," Hades purred, unaffected by Cadmus' tone. "Why do you feel so threatened by me? I was simply reminding Harmonia that she does indeed know me. She resided in my palace for several months. There is no need for her to immediately think badly of me or question my motives."

"On the contrary, dark lord," Cadmus retorted as he straightened out of his crouch. "That is precisely the reason why she should question you. She knows you and what you are capable of."

A brief look of annoyance crossed Hades' face before he masked it, as he too straightened. "I have no motive this time," he asserted impatiently. "As I have already stated, I simply don't know which scenario would be best for the Underworld. I will stand aside and allow things to unfold…for now."

I watched him for a moment, trying to decide what to do. Cadmus had fallen into place next to Harmonia and Brennan held my hand. Hades turned, his dark eyes scorching my own.

"Make the decision, Empusa," he implored. "Only you can decide. What shall it be? Death and destruction for the mortal world or will you master your abilities and save them all?"

He seemed to almost enjoy the predicament that I was in and all of a sudden, it hit me. *He did.* He was just like the other Olympians. Eons of the sameness had rendered him bored. This was something out of the ordinary and that meant that it was interesting to him. He didn't truly care which way it ended, with an apocalypse or otherwise. He simply sought the entertainment.

He winked at me. "And I thought Harmonia knew me," he observed. "Maybe it is you that knows me better."

"You're pathetic," I told him quietly. "How could you not care what happened to them? They haven't done anything to you. They have lives and families."

"We all have our burdens to bear," he answered lightly, moving past my barb with ease. "Empusa, there is so much more at stake here than pitiful mortal families. The entire world could hang in the balance, really." He sounded excited and hopeful and the way he phrased it caused a light to turn on in my head.

"You'd like an apocalypse," I said slowly. "You're not indifferent at all. If every mortal soul was sent here to you, than Zeus would no longer have a kingdom other than the gods in the Spiritlands. And with every mortal soul in the world moved to the Underworld, you think you would be more powerful."

"Why, of course I would be," Hades drawled, his face impossibly calm and serene. "But that isn't my motive, dear one. And it really all hinges on you, anyway. If you can master your own abilities, the world won't end and all of your precious mortal souls will remain in their world. If you can't… well, alas, they will be sent to me. Their fates rest on your shoulders, my dear, not mine."

And I knew he was right. He would benefit if I failed, but it wouldn't be his fault. If I failed and caused an apocalypse in the mortal world, it would be no one's fault but my own.

"You have forgotten one important aspect," I reminded him grimly. "The only reason that the mortal world would be in danger at all is if Brennan and I try to be together. If we stay apart then there is nothing to fear."

I wanted to double over with my words as my stomach constricted. Brennan's gaze was desperate as he sought mine, but the brief panic that I saw in Hades' face was worth it.

It seemed that we had just found leverage against the god of the Underworld.

# Chapter Eighteen

The night hung heavily within my bedroom. My balcony doors were open, allowing the fragrant breeze of the Isles of the Blessed to ruffle the sheer drapes that hung on each side of the door. Shadows from the moon slanted across the walls and I watched them morph and change shape at the same time as I tried to absorb the moon's energy.

I was alone for the first time today. Cadmus wanted to show Brennan the bath house, but I knew it was simply an excuse for Cadmus to speak with him. I hoped that Cadmus would share some of his wisdom that he had gleaned over the years, both as a king of Thebes and as the husband to a goddess.

Hades had retreated to his own palace in the Erebus region of the Underworld and Harmonia was putting Raquel to bed. The dead did not sleep, but she was supposed to at least rest. I was resting myself, although I wasn't able to sleep, either. There was simply too much to think about.

"You should rest, sweet one," a quiet voice said from the doorway.

I glanced up to find Harmonia standing quietly as she watched me struggle with my thoughts. Her face was lovely and serene, awash with the silver light of the moon.

"How do you always stay so calm?" I grumbled curiously. "I feel as though I could run a marathon fueled simply from nervous energy. Yet you are as cool and calm as can be. How do you do that? Tell me your secret."

Harmonia laughed, a tinkling, light sound that seemed to echo in the quiet room. It was a delicate sound that matched her perfectly.

"Empusa, who are you talking to? I'm the goddess of peace. Of course I reflect that. And usually, I help inspire peace in those around me. But not you, not today. Your spirit is too troubled. But I think I can help."

She padded quietly to the side of the large bed and perched on the edge, her emerald silk nightgown dragging softly behind her on the smooth stone. Her slim shoulder was warm against mine and she held out her wrist.

"Here," she suggested. "I know that you must be hungry. You are very pale. You need blood."

Alarm shot through me, causing my heart to race. "I need mortal blood," I clarified. "You're not mortal. And those are the terms of my curse—I must take mortal souls and drink mortal blood."

"Sweet, sweet Empusa," Harmonia shook her head slightly as she pushed her wrist directly under my nose.

Her skin smelled like honeysuckle and was as smooth as silk. My mouth watered at the thought, a subconscious reaction. I cringed away. "Empusa, surely you have learned by now that all is not what it seems, correct? The gods don't always tell you everything."

I stared at her questioningly. "What do you mean?"

She shook her arm toward me once more, throwing the scent of her skin into the air. I inhaled it, closing my eyes.

"I mean, you can drink my blood and not only will you receive more energy than you would if I was mortal, but you will also be infused with my peace. It will help calm you and my goddess powers will combine with yours to make you temporarily stronger."

My eyes popped open. "Such a thing is possible?" I breathed. I had been alive for a thousand years and I had never come across this bit of knowledge before?

Harmonia nodded. "Of course it is. Anything is possible. It is not something to trifle with, however. As you are aware, our abilities are powerful and difficult to contain at times. You must use caution."

My eyes met hers and I found her to be as sincere a person as I'd ever met. Her vibrant jade green eyes held warmth, compassion and grace. I nodded slowly. "Thank you for telling me."

"Now drink," she instructed. "My arm grows tired waiting." She laughed again and I felt a slight thrill course through me. Nervous energy once again. The knowledge that I would be stronger if I drank Harmonia's blood buoyed me. And thrilled me. I couldn't deny it. It was an intoxicating thought.

"But use caution, young one," she murmured again as she watched my face and read my mind. "When you and Brennan do this, it will be entirely different. Your powers are conflicting and will be very hard to contain. But this will be good practice for you."

I grew still as I froze, holding her limp wrist in my hand.

"What do you mean, when Brennan and I do this?"

Harmonia stared at me in surprise. "When you share blood," she clarified. "How else did you think that you would combine your power?"

I swallowed, feeling foolish. We thought that we'd have to have sex to channel that energy in each other. Harmonia read my mind and smiled.

"Well, that might be more fun, I'll admit," she said impishly. "But no. This is the way to do it correctly. And it is very dangerous, which is why I'm letting you practice with me. Drink, young one. My energy is calm and peaceful. It should be easy for you to manage it."

She was right. I could already feel it in the air. Simply being around Harmonia created an atmosphere of peace. I knew that drinking it in would be even better. Without further hesitation, I drew her hand to my mouth and bit, my teeth sinking quickly into the softness of her skin.

Her blood was warm and fragrant and tasted like sweet peas and honeysuckle, exactly like she smelled.

As I drank, I literally felt calm descend upon me like a fog and I sighed happily. Harmonia smiled slightly as she patiently allowed me to drink.

After another minute, she patted my shoulder. "That's enough, young one. You've had plenty for now."

Reluctantly, I pulled away…something that was surprisingly hard to do. I found that I already craved the serenity that her blood provided. As I moved, though, I recognized a physical difference. I did feel calmer, stronger and more sure of myself. Harmonia recognized it too and nodded.

"You're stronger," she observed. "I see it in your eyes and you have color in your cheeks. Focus on that strength. Pull it up from your gut and do something with it. Show me that you can control it."

I lifted my hands and I felt the strength in my fingertips. They practically buzzed with feather-light electricity.

"Show me," Harmonia encouraged.

Glancing at her, I rose from the bed and padded softly to the balcony doors. Gazing down onto the courtyard below, I searched for something to do, some way to practice my temporarily enhanced power.

There was a fountain in the center of the gardens, a likeness of Athena swinging a sword. I focused on her smooth marble face and within a minute, she had broken free from the stone pedestal base, straightening from her combative pose and sheathing the sword at her side.

"Impressive," Harmonia said softly at my side. "But not really impressive enough. You could have done that without my blood. Think bigger."

She was right. I could easily have redesigned the statue on my own. It wasn't that difficult. I studied my surroundings again. On the edge of the lawns, a large raven sat, his head cocked slightly as he watched me with glittering crimson eyes.

Brennan and Cadmus emerged on the other side of the courtyard, their hair still wet from the bath house. I glanced at them and an idea came to me.

Quickly, before I could think the better of it, I focused on Cadmus, then on the bird. I pictured their hearts beating, synchronizing. In my mind's eye, I saw their blood pulsing through their veins. Energy flowed through me, filling my veins and welling in my chest until it felt like it exploded with my effort.

Cadmus stopped still in his tracks, a blank look on his handsome, bronzed face. Brennan gazed at him curiously.

"Are you alright?" he asked Cadmus.

Cadmus looked at him silently, his eyes wide and puzzled. He opened his mouth and nothing came out. He opened it once more… and cawed loudly.

From across the lawns, the raven was walking in a circle, lifting each leg pluckily.

"What the hell?" it asked bluntly in Cadmus' deep voice.

I stared at them in astonishment. I had managed to switch their souls. Cadmus was inside the raven and he didn't look happy about it.

"Now *that's* impressive," Harmonia commended me, patting my shoulder. "But you'd better switch them back before Cadmus kills me."

I knew Cadmus would never in a million years lay a finger on her, but I squinted my eyes and focused on doing what she asked. Within a few seconds, they were back to normal. Cadmus patted his arms and legs as if to make sure and then strode across the courtyard toward me.

"Uh-oh," I muttered, taking an unconscious step backward. Harmonia laughed.

"Don't worry," she assured me. "I'm certain he found it humorous."

The dark, thunderous look on his face contradicted her statement, however, and I waited for a lecture. He retreated into the palace and I waited for him to reemerge in my bedchambers. It only took him a minute. I stood silently in front of him, my head ducked just slightly.

Cadmus used one finger and lifted my chin, making me look him in the eyes.

"That was interesting, Empusa," he said with a humoring grin. "But don't do it again, alright? I hate birds." He shook his head in disgust, presumably remembering how it felt to be inside of one. I laughed and pushed his arm as Brennan walked up.

"That was really impressive, Em," he said in appreciation, his hazel eyes warm. "How did you do that?"

"Harmonia," I explained simply. "Harmonia explained a few things. The way to enhance our powers is through our blood. I tried it with Harmonia. I am strangely at peace right now even though our situation is so tenuous. Her blood infused mine with serenity and I'm twice as strong as I was."

"And if you would join with Brennan in such a way, your strength would be even greater," Harmonia interrupted. "Much greater, actually."

"But I don't understand," Brennan asked in confusion. "I thought our energy was going to automatically become out of control if we simply stay together. Why would we need to trigger that with our blood?"

"You're right," Harmonia explained patiently. "Your combined energy will become out of control with just being together. The way to harness it is through your blood. That is how you will strengthen you bond and hopefully overcome that problem."

"Circes said I should never drink from your blood," Brennan remembered uncertainly. "Remember, Em? She said that your life could depend on it…that we wouldn't be able to control the power it unleashed."

"She said that I would risk everything for you," I corrected. "She didn't say that my life would be threatened by sharing energy."

"Wait," Harmonia broke in. "You've already spoken with Circes and she cautioned you against being together?"

I nodded.

"Then it is unlikely that she will help you," Harmonia pointed out. "But truly, perhaps you don't need her help after all. You know what you need to do. The only thing left for you to do is to practice…in a safe place."

"You're not worried about Circes' reservations?" Brennan asked her incredulously. Harmonia returned his gaze calmly.

"Brennan, you will soon discover that there are times in this world when you can only trust your own instincts. Many people around you might have ulterior motives. I don't know if Circes does… or if she doesn't. But I know what I feel in my heart. When I see the way you look at Empusa and the way she returns your gaze, I know that whatever you have is worth fighting for. Trust me, this is something I know: There is nothing worse in all the world than saying goodbye to your soul mate."

Cadmus stroked her arm lightly and I could see the love on his face. It was heart-warming, particularly when I knew how many times they'd been forced to say goodbye over the years. They had certainly earned their Happily-Ever-After.

"We're together now, my love," he told her softly, bending to kiss her gently. "I'll never leave your side again."

Harmonia wrapped her arms around his neck and held him tightly to her heart for a moment. "You'll never have to leave me again," she reminded him. "All that we will ever need is right here."

They smiled into each other's eyes and my heart constricted once more from the warmth that they exuded.

"You both are very blessed," I told them, speaking around the heavy knot that had formed in my throat.

"And so too will you be," Cadmus assured me, his face sincere. "You already are, little one. You've found your soul mate. Many, many people search for eons and never find what you already have right before you. So you see, you are blessed as well."

And I was. Looking at Brennan, at his kind, gentle smile, I knew that was true.

"We can do this," I told Brennan softly. "Cadmus is right. We have each other and that's really all we need. I have faith in that."

"Then so do I," he replied, reaching out to grasp my hand. His long fingers encircled mine and I closed my eyes, enjoying the way my hand fit within his.

The familiarity of Brennan's touch caused warmth to swell in my heart where a deep satisfaction grew. The warmth filled me up and exploded from my fingertips, shocking me with its sudden eruption. The glass balcony doors behind me shattered, the jagged pieces flying around us. I stared at them in astonishment.

"That's just a small example of what you could happen when you're together," Harmonia said quietly.

"But we weren't even doing anything," I protested. "I was just enjoying how Brennan held my hand and then—"

"Exactly," Cadmus interrupted grimly. "You weren't even doing anything. You certainly weren't trying to channel Brennan's energy, yet you did. It's a subconscious thing for you. You will both have to work hard to overcome it."

"Yes," I agreed, scanning the face of everyone surrounding me. "I know. And I'll do it. We'll both work harder than we've ever worked at anything, won't we, Brennan?"

He nodded stoically. "Absolutely. Because you're worth it."

I looked into his eyes in time to see them turn from hazel to butterscotch with determination. My heart warmed again at the tender look on his face and the chandelier in the bedroom shattered into a million pieces.

I stared at its bare skeleton as it swung frantically above us and sighed.

We had a lot of work to do.

# Chapter Nineteen

"I think we should have stayed with Harmonia and Cadmus in the Underworld," Brennan said nervously as he pivoted in a circle, examining our surroundings. "It's too much pressure to be back in the mortal world, Em. What if we accidentally hurt someone?"

I sighed, not from impatience, but because I was worried about exactly the same thing. I just didn't want to completely wreck Harmonia's home with our energy and it was unnerving to know that Hades was waiting for the first sign of a mistake.

"That's true, too," Brennan agreed, reading my mind. "That was annoying. He wants us to fail."

"Of course he does," I agreed. "He wants the mortal world to end. He wants all of those souls and he wants, once and for all, to finally overtake Zeus for good. It's all he's ever truly wanted."

Brennan shook his head and stared at the ground below us, wiggling his toes over the side of the cliff we were standing on.

"But why Death Valley?" he asked curiously. "Why did you want to come here? It's the most extreme place on earth, I think."

"And that's exactly why I wanted to come here," I said softly, staring at the ground below us. "It is extremely remote. So much of it is isolated and desolate, but there is beauty here. Amidst all of the barren nothingness, there is beauty. You just have to look for it."

The terrain around us was windswept and barren. Hardened sand ripples had formed in the ground, seemingly rippling over the edge of the far horizon. Jagged hills rolled for miles, abrupt and severe, forming angular valleys that were shielded from the elements. There was no one around for miles…the perfect place for us to be.

"I can see your point," Brennan acknowledged. "And there *is* beauty here." With his words, he reached out and touched my face, sliding his fingers down my cheek to the hollow of my neck.

I smiled but didn't take my attention away from the landscape in front of us. It had never been more important that we stay focused. Brennan replied to my unspoken thought.

"You're right. I'm sorry. I'll be good," he promised, removing his hand from my neck. I felt the absence of his warmth immediately and I longed to have it back. But now wasn't the time.

"How do we know where we should go?" Brennan asked curiously as he studied the land below us with me. "I know that you can conjure up shelter anywhere. So does it really matter?"

"Yes," I answered absently. "You forget that Mormo is still hunting us. We'll need somewhere with good vantage points where we can see him coming."

"But you have your bracelet back, so that should help somewhat," Brennan pointed out.

"It will help, yes," I replied. "But it only gives us a scant moment's notice. I'd prefer to have a little more of a head's up than that. Look over there. It looks like a little canyon filled with rock formations. I think we should go there. There's protection from the elements, we can make a camp on a ledge higher up in the canyon… it should work."

Brennan followed my pointing finger and gazed at the red rocks in the distance before he nodded. "Yep, it should work." He held out his hand. "Shall we?"

I smiled and grasped his strong fingers, closing my eyes. I pictured the exact place where I wanted to make camp in my mind and when I re-opened my eyes, we were there.

"I'm glad I'm not afraid of heights," Brennan said wryly as he stared downward from the ledge we were perched on.

We were hundreds of yards above the ground, on a stone ledge that was only four feet wide. Small pebbles and red rock dust swept across the stone, but that was it.

Nothing grew here on the rock. Other shale ledges above us provided shade, which would be nice when the sun was at its peak in the afternoon. It grew very hot here in Death Valley in the day time and then very cold at night. It was a place that could be very dangerous simply because of the elements.

I stared at the back corner of the ledge and squinted. A tent appeared, already assembled. I blinked once and the inside was filled with warm sleeping bags, air mattresses, pillows and an ice chest full of food and water. Brennan stared at me in appreciation.

"Have I ever told you that you're handy to have around?"

I laughed and shrugged.

"Brennan, this is something that you can do as well. Or, I guess I should say that it is something you will be able to do someday when you have mastered it. All it takes is practice. I've had a thousand years of practice, so I'm a little ahead of you."

"You know," he replied thoughtfully. "It makes sense that you're my soul mate. I've always been into older chicks. They're just more mature."

I laughed again. "I think being with me is slightly different than dating someone a year ahead of you in school. But like I told you before... time is nothing, Brennan. Pretty soon, it will fade away and you'll see for yourself."

"But what about my father?" he asked in concern. "I'll have to watch him die, won't I?"

I stilled for a moment at this turn in conversation. There were times, because I'd been around for so long, that I had forgotten how to empathize with human emotion. Of course this issue would be troubling for Brennan and I hadn't even thought about it. I chose my words carefully.

"Yes. You'll have to watch your mortal father die. But we'll have to discuss how to handle that particular situation a little later. He can't know about you... what you are. If you choose immortality and choose to live with me forever, you will stop aging. There will come a point when you won't be able to visit him any longer, you'll have to watch him from afar. Do you think you can do that?"

Brennan's eyes clouded over and I knew he was thinking of his father.

"He's already lost so much," Brennan said softly, gazing into the distance without actually seeing it. "My mother, his brother. And now me. But he's strong. I know he will be fine. I choose you, Empusa."

He turned to look at me, his hazel eyes appearing as gold in the sun. "I choose you," he said again. The way he said it troubled me.

"I'm not asking you to choose between me and your mortal life," I said slowly. "I'm truly not. If I had my way, you could have everything in the world that you wanted. But this is one limitation that we have. We can't maintain a life in the mortal world and one in immortality. It just doesn't work that way. It makes my heart hurt to see the pain on your face when you think of losing him, Brennan. You need to carefully consider this. Very, very carefully."

"But you lived in the mortal world," Brennan recalled, his forehead wrinkled. "Why can't we linger here?"

"We could," I shrugged. "But what you don't realize now, because you've never been to the Spiritlands, is that living here only allows us to be a shadow of our true selves. So much is possible when we're at home where we belong. We don't have to hide who we are. You'll see. If that's what you choose," I added quickly.

"I choose that," he confirmed firmly. "I will always choose you, Empusa. That's not even a question."

A part of me that I didn't even know was there, a small, insecure place, felt instantly soothed with his words. I hadn't even known that I was uneasy, but now I felt comforted. If he would choose me over his mortal life, over his own mortal father, then I knew he would choose me over anything else that would come.

He stood and balanced on the edge of the stone shelf. "I've never been to Death Valley before," he said, changing the subject as he gazed around us in wonderment. "I thought it would be all desert sand."

I stood and held his hand as we looked below us. In between rolling hills and mounds of rocks, acres of dark pink flowers grew, their vibrant green foliage waving in the breeze. The air was hot but dry and the breeze felt nice as it rustled my hair away from my face.

"No, it is not all sand here," I replied. "I believe that Death Valley is the hottest, driest and lowest place in the United States. It is rugged and dangerous, but I think that's why I like it. That makes it exciting. It's beautiful, but deadly."

"Like you," Brennan observed with a small smile.

"Like me," I acknowledged with a sigh.

As I spoke, a movement from the corner of my eye caught my attention and I turned. A large black dog sat on its haunches in the distance watching us. Its ears were at attention, its eyes focused unwaveringly upon us.

"That's a really big dog," Brennan said with a laugh. "I wonder what it's doing all the way out here by itself?"

I stared at it again, watching the way the dog's eyes connected with mine before I sighed.

"It's my mother," I told him reluctantly. "Her familiar is a black dog. She uses it sometimes in the mortal world when she wants to be inconspicuous."

"Your mother is a dog?" Brennan asked, grinning. "Your family just gets curiouser and curiouser, Em."

"Don't I know it," I said, rolling my eyes. "I don't know why she's sitting all the way over there. She's keeping an eye on me. She might as well do it from here."

I waved at her and the dog cocked its head, but remained in place.

"I think she still wants to give you space," Brennan suggested. "She probably knows that you're still upset with her."

"Of course I'm still upset with her!" I snapped. "She tied my soul to a jewel. Who does that? How could she not have seen what problems it would cause?"

Brennan studied me thoughtfully. "Who does that? Not normal families for sure... but your family isn't normal. Your mother is the goddess of witchcraft. And maybe you're right. Maybe she just got a little too big for her boots because she's handled so much power for so long. But I'm sure that she didn't mean any harm. She only wants to protect you. I don't even know her and I know that."

"I know," I said simply. "But I can't help how I feel, Brennan."

I blinked my eyes back toward the horizon to find that my mother was gone. But I knew that she wasn't very far away. She was clearly here to watch me, so I knew that was exactly what she was going to do. And I had to admit, the knowledge that she was near was comforting.

"Okay, so we're here for a purpose," Brennan said uncertainly. "But I feel strange doing something so intimate with you when I know that your mother is watching us."

I smiled. "I know. But that's something that you'll have to get accustomed to. When you live in a world where your mind can be read, your thoughts are not private. It's just something you learn to live with."

"It's not really my thoughts I was concerned about," Brennan muttered and I had to laugh.

"You know we're not having sex right now, right?" I asked with another laugh. "There's no way we could handle that kind of power right now. We'd lose focus and maybe take out the Eastern Seaboard."

"The Eastern Seaboard?" Brennan gasped in mock outrage as he clutched at his chest dramatically. "Not the Eastern Seaboard! And I've always held such a special place in my heart for... New Jersey. Or Rhode Island."

We laughed, but only to cover up our nervousness. He had made a valid point. It would be strange to partake in any kind of intimacy while we knew my mother was watching. As if to prove that we could do it, he pulled me to him and I melted into his strong embrace. I fit so perfectly in his arms.

He lowered his lips to mine and gently kissed me. I wrapped my arms around his neck and leaned into him, deepening the kiss. My heart slammed in my chest from his nearness, something that always seemed to happen. I heard a roaring in my ears but ignored it as I allowed his mouth to ravage mine, my fingers clutching at his strong chest.

After a few minutes, I came up for air. When I did, I realized that the roaring hadn't been in my ears. Our tent was in flames, the orange and red fingers scorching at the sky. I dropped my head, stepped away from Brennan and sighed.

"It seems that we have a lot of work to do," I murmured dejectedly as I conjured water to douse the fire with. Brennan gazed at the charred remains of our little shelter, the burned edges of the tent flapping in the breeze.

"We did that?" he asked incredulously. "Just by kissing?"

"I'm afraid so," I replied tiredly. "Just by kissing. The more you develop your powers, the more our energy reacts to each other. We've got to get a handle on it."

"There's no time like the present, then," Brennan said determinedly as he grasped my hand. I nodded in agreement.

"You're right. There's no time like the present."

I focused on clearing off the charred mess of our tent and replacing it with a clean, new shelter filled with everything that we would need. Bending, I pushed through the new tent flap and pulled Brennan inside with me. Stretching out on the plush sleeping bag, I patted the ground next to me. Brennan slid next to me.

"Now what?" he asked nervously. "I don't want to hurt you."

I had to laugh at that. "You could never hurt me," I answered confidently. "I'm certain about that."

He groaned and pulled me to him. "I won't. I promise," he growled, clutching me tightly to his chest. I felt both fragile and protected within his arms and I was reluctant to leave his embrace. But it was necessary.

Backing up, I slid my teeth along the soft skin of my wrist, creating a short slice in my arm. I held it out to him at the same time as he offered me his own. Without hesitation, I bit, drinking in his warm, mortal blood. Instant strength and light flooded my limbs as mind-shattering sensations enveloped me. His blood tasted just the same as it did last time...like no other. I drank for a few minutes before I opened my eyes to look at Brennan.

His eyes were wide and stricken as my blood streaked down his chin. He gazed past me toward something that I couldn't see. I pulled my wrist away from his mouth and clutched at his shoulders.

"Brennan, what is it?" I asked quickly, stroking his back. "Are you alright? What's wrong?"

He turned to me, his tanned face pale, his fingers shaky. "You were right, Em. The world's going to end and it's going to be our fault."

# Chapter Twenty

"The world is not going to end," I insisted slowly, taking in the desperation on Brennan's stricken face. "Why would you think so? I was wrong when I said it would, Brennan. We can prevent my visions. We can do anything we set our minds to."

Brennan turned to me, his expression slightly calmer than it had been a scant moment ago. I reached out to grab his hand, but he backed away, causing my heart to race. He stepped out of the tent and I trailed behind him quickly.

"What is it?" I whispered. "What did you see, Brennan?"

His eyes were pain-filled and stark when he answered. "I saw flames and floods and a lot of blood. There was so much blood. I saw the same things that you did, Empusa. And if we both see it, I think it is likely to happen."

"It won't!" I cried, gritting my teeth and throwing myself at him. Clutching at him, I gripped his shoulders, trying to make him touch me. Yet he still shirked away from my fingers like I had a sickness. It was alarming.

"Why are you moving away from me?" I asked helplessly, trying to ignore the cold pit growing in my belly. "I didn't cause your visions, Brennan. I wish nothing more than to protect you from any ugliness in the world."

"I know," he admitted softly. "But I also know that this isn't going to work."

His voice was like gravel, painfully scraping the surface of my heart with every husky syllable. "I can't be with you," he repeated.

He was so casual, so perfunctory, as though we were simply talking about a Cubs game or the weather. I stared at him, at his flecked hazel eyes that gleamed in the sunlight and my chest literally constricted at the thought of even one day without him.

"Yes, you can. You're perfect for me," I answered uncertainly, reaching for him, trying to pull him close. If he could just feel my heart pressed against his, I knew that he might bend, if only just enough to listen. But he would have none of it and backed away, leaning against the rocks behind us. He knew the danger within my touch.

"Brennan," I tried again, stepping forward. The way that the sun bathed him in backlit glory was breath-taking and I had to re-focus. It was difficult not to concentrate on his handsome, rugged face and the way his mouth moved as he spoke.

"Em," he continued, as if I'd never even spoken. "I'm not...I'm not strong enough for this yet. I won't be able to control my abilities- I just saw it. I can't jeopardize the entire mortal world simply because I can't master my power. And Circes... she said that you would risk everything for me. I can't allow that, Empusa. I can't be the one who extinguishes your light. That won't be me."

He pushed away from the rocks and strode down the ledge with his distinctive lope. He paused just once on the edge, before he bounded, landing gracefully on his feet far below me. He didn't look back, he simply walked away from me. I stood still, frozen by his words, astounded by their meaning. Until I realized that if I didn't do something right now I would never see him again.

I lunged from the ledge, landing roughly in the packed sand below before I raced along behind him. Even employing supernatural speed, I didn't catch up with him for a mile. He had mastered speed himself, it seemed. Out of the corner of my eye, I saw a flash of black and I knew that my mother was close, watching us, but it didn't sway me.

I pushed Brennan against a nearby red stone rock mound, shoving him hard and he stumbled, staring at me in shock as his back collided with the stone. He had never seen me lose my temper. No one had. I always had to be so careful, so controlled.

"You think it's only up to you?" I shouted. The wind whipped my hair around my face and I ignored it as I stared directly into the mesmerizing eyes of the only man I had ever loved.

"I have a say in this, too," I insisted. "You think you can just throw everything away with a handful of cliches? Newsflash: The old *it's not you, it's me* line isn't effective. If you don't want to be with me, just be man enough to tell me why. Don't tell me that it is because of the visions. We can overcome them. I know it. If there is something else, tell me right now."

My face was barely an inch from his. I was close enough to feel his heart beat through his shirt, to feel the heat from his skin pulse through and bleed into my own skin. I was close enough to inhale his very breath. I knew what my nearness would do to him, but I didn't care. I closed my eyes and leaned into him... instantly absorbing what he felt; the jagged pain, the overwhelming uncertainty, but mostly, his unbridled need for me. It filled him up and spilled into me.

"Tell me," I murmured against his lips.

He groaned and pulled me against him, his large hands flattening against my back as he smashed me to his chest and ravaged my lips with his own. He kissed me like the world was ending. And I knew, with every breath in me, that if he left, my world *would* end.

His body was rock hard and he smelled like the sun. I inhaled him as I grasped his hair and pulled him closer to me, as close as I could possibly get. Even in the heat of this moment, though, I had to keep a corner of my consciousness carefully focused, making sure I didn't absorb too much of his strength.  But I still allowed myself to taste it, to enjoy it.

He was delicious.  Everything about him.

His tongue rammed into my mouth, swirling with mine and he tasted like honey as his very life flowed into me, wispy and transparent, but pulsing hard.  He was so *vital.*

It made me wild and I couldn't control myself.  I ripped at his shirt, breaking the buttons as I frantically pushed it off of his shoulders.  I knew it was expensive, but I didn't care.  My only thought was consuming all of him, every bit and I needed him inside of me to do that. It was the only way.  My focus faltered and then was obliterated.  Nothing else mattered now but my need for him.

I began seeing things in blurs of color, tasting the scents in the air and feeling the textures beneath my hands as everything else faded away. His breathing was ragged, his heart beat stuttering and racing as we fumbled with clothing.  Our skin was hot and sticky as we pressed together.  I felt his heart beat join with mine, synching perfectly, as the process began.  My fingers pulsed and my vision unfocused.  It was happening.  I would only need a moment longer.

Out of the corner of my eye, I saw the beautiful field of pink flowers explode into flame, too close to withstand my energy as it flared into an uncontrollable storm. They burned impotently against the sandy horizon as our very own fire burned within us. A loud boom exploded somewhere nearby and I saw chunks of earth scatter, falling around us from the sky. I had no idea where it had come from and I didn't care at this point.

Brennan yanked at the button on his pants and I reached to help him, desperate to continue, to finish, but somehow sanity returned to me as I thought of that very word.

*Finish.*

If we completed this act, if I made love to this man- the man that I loved with every ounce of my being, it would finish him. He could die because we hadn't learned to master our power.

I froze.

He reached for me, but I held out my hand.

"Don't," I rasped uncomfortably. "Give me a minute."

I closed my eyes, willing my heart beat to calm, to slow, even as I willed myself to ignore the raging fire that had overtaken me the second his life had filled my mouth. This was my curse and I almost always won. I couldn't afford to lose control with him. Not with him.

I opened my eyes a few minutes later, exhaling a long exasperated sigh.

"I'm sorry."

He stared at me from a few feet away, his hazel eyes calm. His thumbs were looped through his belt loops and he stood casually, as if he hadn't almost just died at my hands.

"I know," he answered softly. "But this… this is why. Em, your mother was right. Together we are very, very dangerous. To each other and to everyone else in the world. Look behind you."

I turned to find that we had created some sort of unnatural geyser. The earth around us had ripped apart and a geyser had erupted, shooting hot water from deep in the earth high in the sky above us. It landed in fat droplets around us, sizzling in the heat as it ran off the dry ground in hot streams.

"Em, I love you. But I don't see this ending well. I can't control myself around you and you get carried away when you are with me. How can that possibly end well? How can we ever learn to control such a thing?"

I heard the words and I knew he was right. Once I cast my innate spell, something that was even stronger when I was aroused, any man who I was with couldn't resist me. They couldn't think the better of it, even when they knew that being with me would kill them. And once the process had gotten to a certain point, I couldn't control it either. One of these times, it would go too far and I would drain every ounce of life from his body before we could stop ourselves.

I swallowed hard, my gray eyes frozen on his beautiful, rugged face.

"I can't let you go," I whispered. "I know this is hard. But maybe if we tried harder…" my voice caught in my throat and I turned my head away from him. He didn't need to see me cry.

I felt him step close to me and he turned my chin with a finger. So gently. He was always so gentle with me. I could still feel his life force pulsing, the current flowing directly beneath his skin, but I gritted my teeth and ignored it. I could do this.

"Em," he murmured. "I want nothing more than to be with you. Every day, every night, forever."

He paused and stared into my eyes. So close to me again, so trusting, so alive. I could hear his heart beating in his chest and I felt sweat form on my brow. I ground my teeth harder. I could do this. I wouldn't hurt him. I automatically took a step back. *I wouldn't hurt him.*

"Can you promise me that you can stop?" he asked. "Because that is the only way we could work. I know that I can't control myself. I'm not strong enough yet. So you'd have to be the one. Can you go against your nature until we figure this out?"

His voice was both pained and painful and I turned my head. I stared away from him at the shooting power of the newly formed geyser. The moisture from it called to me, I could feel it from here. It replenished my energy, revitalized me.

Like men did. Only without men, without their vital energy, their blood...their *souls,* I would die. And Brennan knew that.

"I can't," I whispered harshly.

That wasn't quite true. I could, for a few weeks at the most, but after that, I would quickly age into the ancient old woman that I should be by now. And then I would die.

"I know," he nodded sadly. "And that is my point. We can't have a happily ever after, so what is the sense in it? In all good conscious, how can we risk the entire world on something that we know we will probably fail at?"

My burning eyes filled with tears and I blinked them away. He was right. I knew he was right. But my heart didn't agree. I opened my mouth to speak, then closed it again. What was there to say? He was right. My head dropped and I stared dejectedly at the sand.

For just a scant moment until a vibrant glowing from my bracelet illuminated against the pale skin of my arm and snapped my head up. I gripped my wrist with shaking fingers.

"My father," I stuttered, gazing around quickly. I was shaky and weak from the incident with Brennan, not an ideal time for an encounter with my murderous father.

Brennan immediately crouched into a defensive position in front of me, his alert eyes trained on the horizon. His bare torso was taut and glistened in the sun.

"He won't lay a hand on you. I promise you that, Em."

The protective tone in his voice constricted my heart, but I couldn't dwell on it. Instead, I shifted my attention to the terrain around us. My mother materialized next to me, a shiny dagger in her hand.

"He will *not* touch you. I promise that, as well." Her ivory cloak fluttered softly in the breeze around her, her blonde hair swaying in the wind. She didn't look like a warrior, but I knew that she was very, very deadly. She turned her gaze to me and I saw determination in it.

"Empusa, join hands with Brennan. We're going to need your combined power."

"But mother, we don't know how to harness it yet," I started to protest, but she interrupted me.

"I know that, Em. But I'm here to help you now. Do as I say."

She shoved me forward and I grabbed Brennan's hand. Even in this moment, with danger surrounding us, I enjoyed the feel of his fingers. He squeezed my hand lightly and I knew that he shared the feeling.

"Show yourself, Mormo!" my mother shouted. "We know you're here. And I know that you are not alone. Come out!"

In unison, Brennan and I turned to examine our perimeter, but the only thing moving was red sand blowing along the hardened ground. I couldn't see my father's cursed face anywhere.

"Where are you?" I shouted in frustration. "If you want me, you'll have to come face me. Stop hiding like the coward that you are!"

"That's it, sweetie, antagonize the bad guy," Brennan said wryly without removing his gaze from the horizon.

"I can't help it," I muttered. "He's made my life hell. It needs to end here. I can't take it anymore."

I could hear the pain in my own voice as it caught in my throat and Brennan froze for a second, his gaze meeting mine.

"Empusa… I—" his voice caught as well and he cleared his throat.

"Empusa, I want you to know that I love you. No matter what happens, I love you and I need for you to know that."

I squeezed his hand, almost unable to answer around the lump in my throat. "I know you do, Brennan. I love you too."

"There's time for that later, Empusa," my mother admonished. "I need you to focus now. Do the seeking spell with me."

But before either of us could utter a single word, a circle of women appeared high above us on the ledge of the canyon. Their fierce faces were trained on us, their muscles as large and toned as any man's I'd ever seen. There must have been fifty of them, all dressed in thigh-length tunics and battle armor.

"The Amazons," I breathed, as I focused in on the face of their queen, Ortrera. I'd met her once before in the Underworld when she was there with Harmonia searching for Raquel.

"Harmonia must have sent them, bless her heart," my mother agreed.

I met the gaze of Ortrera and she nodded once in confirmation. Yes, Harmonia had sent them. They were here to help. Each of their arms was drawn back and I realized that they were each holding a bow and arrow, poised to shoot. I felt a tiny bit better. I had the goddess of witchcraft and an Amazon army on my side. My odds were looking up.

"The seeking spell, Empusa," my mother reminded me hurriedly and I nodded. But once again, before we could utter a single word, we were interrupted.

"Empusa," a loud and chilling voice boomed.

We frantically looked around us, but the voice had seemed to come from everywhere... and nowhere. Mormo was still nowhere to be found. I could see the Amazons searching from their higher vantage point, but not a one of us could see him.

"Did you really think you could hide from me, daughter?" the voice boomed again and icy chills shot down my spine, shivering into the depths of my soul. "The bargain that I made with Hades stands until it is changed and you aren't strong enough to follow through with that. Your soul is mine."

Brennan whirled me around and touched his forehead to mine.

"Don't listen to him, Em," he implored me. "Your soul does not belong to him. Are you listening to me? If it belongs to anyone besides you, then I would say that it belongs to me. And I was wrong earlier. I'm never going to let it go. Do you understand? We'll handle whatever happens. Just stay with me. We're strong enough. Fight with me."

I stared at him in confusion. "What changed? Two minutes ago, you said we couldn't be together. And now you want to stay and fight with me?"

He sighed. "We'll talk about this at a... better time, but I can't live without you. I don't care how risky it is. I can't physically do it."

"That's sweet," my mother interrupted, "And I fully believe you, son of Apollo, but this is a conversation best left for later... when someone isn't trying to destroy you."

I swallowed and nodded. My mother was right and Brennan and I both knew it.

"I'll fight with you," I promised him. "I'll fight for you until my dying breath."

"No one is dying today," my mother interrupted again, her voice grim and strong.

*Your mother is right,* a voice said in my head and I recognized it as Ortrera's. My gaze flew to meet her hawkish stare. She sat perched high above me, her body still poised for a fight. *But we need your attention here. Focus and stay strong. There is time for intimate conversation later.*

I nodded in agreement and Ortrera appeared satisfied, returning her attention to the horizon, searching for Mormo…which is exactly what I should be doing. My eyes flitted along every rock, every plane, every hill. But I came up empty. He was nowhere to be found.

"Where is he?" I cried in frustration. "He's here, but he's not."

"Your father has always been as a shadow," my mother said quietly. "He flits in and out of reality as quickly as we walk through it. He's skilled in that way. He is accustomed to balancing between the world of the living and the world of the dead."

"Yes, I do operate very well in the world of the dead," Mormo answered her, his voice still echoing loudly through the hot canyon. "And speaking of the dead, I have someone with me whom you might recognize, daughter."

At his words, someone tumbled into the emptiness in front of us. I squinted to get a better look and gasped as recognition struck me. Gaia was tattered and torn, her hair unkempt and dirty, her gowns ragged and ripped.

"Gaia!" I gasped. Brennan was staring at her in horror and fascination.

"I can see her," he said in amazement. "I am looking at a ghost."

"It's my blood," I told him quickly. "You drank my blood, remember? You can share my gifts until the effects wear off." He nodded quickly as I turned back toward Gaia, preparing to run to her, but my mother held out a hand.

"No, don't," she cautioned. "He won't let you near her."

My gaze met my best friend's and hers was panicked. "Empusa, don't!" she cried. "He's using me to get to you. Don't let him."

At her words, Gaia went flying across the canyon and collided into a mound of rocks as though a giant had kicked her. I sucked my breath in. She was lying motionless in the dirt.

"She's already dead," my mother reminded me. "He can't really hurt her."

Blood trickled from Gaia's mouth and her hand twitched. I flinched.

"Are you certain?" I asked my mother. She nodded. "He can't truly hurt her," she amended. "He can cause her pain, but it won't be lasting. She'll be fine. Don't let him control you with this."

"Your mother doesn't always know as much as she thinks," Mormo boomed. "I will arrange for Gaia's soul to be imprisoned in Tartara, the very blackest of places in the Underworld. She'll be sentenced to spending eternity with the most heinous of souls. Is that how you want your friend to exist?"

I gulped hard. Gaia was terrified of the Underworld and I had always told her that parts of it were wonderful, which was true. Her soul was good and I had known that she wouldn't be sent to Tartara. But I had never considered that my father might arrange for just such a thing to be so.

"Don't let him manipulate you," my mother warned again. "He would need Hades' permission for such a thing. I don't see that happening. I will intervene—"

"Mother, we can't trust anyone anymore," I told her in frustration. "Especially not Hades. Why don't you understand that?"

"Why can't you understand that this is a trick?" she beseeched me. "It won't matter what you do here for Gaia. His plans have already been laid."

"What about Zeus?" I asked quickly as I remembered that my mother had gone to speak with him. "What did he say? Will he help me? Maybe he would intervene for Gaia!"

My mother's face clouded over. "I am not sure of Zeus' intentions," she admitted. "I fear that he might wish to allow events to play out as they will simply so that he can see Hades' true intentions for himself. I doubt he will intervene on your behalf until such things have been made clear. He will want to know for certain."

At her words, Mormo laughed, a chilling and terrifying sound. Out of my periphery, I saw Gaia stand up shakily, her back to the rocks. She perched there uncertainly, not sure of what to do.

"Run!" I implored her. She turned and met my gaze, her eyes frozen on mine. "Run," I told her again. She nodded, her face pale. She closed her eyes briefly and then was gone.

"Did you really think that Zeus would help?" Mormo asked, his voice amused as it came from nowhere. "Zeus only helps when it benefits him. You should know that by now."

It was true. I did know that and I felt my shoulders drop slightly.

"Do not listen to him!" my mother hissed as she raised the dagger threateningly at the empty air in front of us. "That is not true and even if it were, there are ways around everything, Empusa. I have thought of a way that we might separate your soul from your moonstone. We may only need for Hades to reverse the curse…something that he has already pledged to do. Zeus has sworn that he will force Hades to uphold his word."

At her words, Mormo suddenly appeared in the canyon in front of us, a swirling mass of black material as his cloak twisted violently about him like a tornado. When the dust around him settled, I stared into the eyes of my father for the first time in a long time…the eyes that were so like mine, yet still so different.

"It matters not!" he roared, his face contorting violently. "I will prevail. This will end today, woman!"

My mother stepped forward, her beautiful face a determined mask. She almost seemed to relish this moment and I realized that she probably did. She had been frustrated by her love for Mormo for a very long time. Perhaps she secretly wanted to end it. If he were to die, she would no longer be tortured by her conflicting feelings.

They marched toward each other, quickly closing the distance between them. I sucked in my breath. Somehow I knew that this wouldn't end well. They couldn't go head to head. Not right now.

"Brennan," I murmured quietly. "Hold tight to my hand. We need to channel our energy. Focus. I want to create a geyser between them, one like we created earlier." He nodded and we both closed our eyes in unison. I imagined the thick earth breaking apart and erupting into a liquid explosion.

The strength of our energy pulsed in my veins, flowing from me to Brennan and back again in a continuous circle. Everyone had been correct. Our energy was powerful. The sensations that it created were almost too strong to bear, too overwhelming. But they were effective.

As my mother strode toward my father, the ground in front of her broke into pieces, shooting toward the sky and throwing her backward. She watched in amazement as the earth continued to crack in a deafening, splitting sound.

"We need to stop," I said frantically, yanking my hand away. The cracking ceased, but not before it had broken apart in a trench that was miles long. Pieces of earth and gravel fell into the deep crevice. Beneath my feet, the earth started to shake and my eyes flew to Brennan's.

"Earthquake," he said unnecessarily. "We must have disturbed a fault line."

I stared helplessly at him as we both recalled our visions. In each of our nightmarish prophecies, we had seen that everything had started with a massive earthquake. My heart started pounding.

"We can't let this happen," I murmured, reaching out for him once again. But before our fingers could touch, I was wrenched away and thrown across the canyon by an unseen force. Momentum carried me farther than I would have liked and I dug my feet into the hard ground to try and stop. But it was no avail, I skidded right over the edge of the newly formed deep crevice. I threw my hands up and grabbed the edge, my fingernails digging into the packed sand.

I glanced below me and saw that the crevice in the earth was deeper than I had even imagined. I could see thick, flowing hot magma beneath me and I cringed. This did not bode well.

"Hold on, Empusa," Gaia implored me. She had appeared at my side in a flash, her ghostly face glowing against the dark, jagged cliff. "Don't let him win, Empusa. Don't let it happen. I know you're tired, but you are strong enough. Pull yourself up."

She floated beside me in the air, her ghostly feet dangling.

"Easy for you to say," I muttered as my arms began to shake. She grinned an eerie grin.

"Just do it," she implored. "Pull up every ounce of strength that you've got and use it right now."

Out of my vision range, I heard Brennan shouting for me. I gritted my teeth and focused. I didn't have enough mental strength to simply materialize elsewhere, so I would have to use physical strength. My arms ached and trembled and I expelled my breath slowly, allowing it to slide over my teeth. I didn't know if I could do this. I didn't know if I was strong enough.

*You are strong enough,* I heard in my head. Brennan. The only voice that mattered right now. *Hold on. I'll be right there.*

I focused, staring at the way my fingers were digging into the hardened clay high above me. I focused on the red hot pain in my shoulders as the muscle pulled away from the bone.

And then Brennan's face appeared above me, as beautiful as anything I'd ever seen. He grasped my wrists and within a second, he had pulled me up and out of harm's way. I clutched him to me and he scooped me into his arms. I barely even felt the pain from my dislocated shoulders. I knew I would heal. All that mattered was that I was here... with Brennan.

"We've got to go," he breathed as he began to run with me in his arms. I stared around him to see my mother fighting Mormo in hand to hand combat. Her dagger whizzed past his head as her leg swung around and kicked his own from beneath him. The Amazons were quickly approaching them to assist.

My mother met my gaze. "Run," she said. "I'll find you. Brennan knows where. Stay safe."

"I love you," I mouthed to her.

"I love you, too," she replied, before Mormo slammed into her with full strength. She returned her attention to him, holding him at bay while the Amazons closed in around them. Geysers shot from the ground around them as she threw Mormo off with supernatural power. Her eyes shifted from blue to silver as she concentrated and I knew she would be alright.

"Where are we going?" I asked Brennan as he moved even faster, carrying us away from Mormo and the danger surrounding us.

Brennan readjusted my weight to hand me a small velvet bag. I peered inside it as he continued running and found a little pile of stone squares.

"Runes?"

He nodded as the countryside around us blurred into nothingness. "Your mother said you could read them… and they would tell us where to go."

I blinked. "It's not so much of a *where* as a *when*. Brennan, do you trust me?"

He gazed down at me, his eyes a dark butterscotch. "Em, I trust you with my life. Whatever happens, I want it to happen with you at my side. We can handle it. We can handle anything."

"Truly?"I asked softly, tracing the outline of his handsome face with my fingers.

"Truly," he confirmed. "I am nothing without you, Emmie. That's something that I know now."

"No," I argued softly, snuggling against his hard chest, relaxing as he ran. "You are everything. *Time* is nothing. You're about to find that out firsthand, I'm afraid."

"I'm not afraid," he said firmly and his tone warmed my heart. "If I'm with you, there's nothing to be afraid of. Being away from you is the only real fear that I have."

I closed my eyes as I pressed my ear to his heart, listening to its powerful beat. "Me too," I admitted softly. "Me too."

But as I allowed his strong legs to carry both of us toward our future, I knew that we didn't need to fear it. We'd never be apart again, no matter what our future held. We were together now and that was how it was going to stay.

In the far distance behind us, an explosion of light sprayed into the sky and I knew that my mother and Mormo were still fighting. But I wasn't afraid. My mother was the strongest witch in the world. She would come out on top and then she would find us. I had faith that everything would be fine. It had to be. It would be. I would make sure of it.

"Hold my hand," I murmured to Brennan. He stopped moving and gazed into my eyes.

"Now? Why?"

"Do you trust me?" I asked, my eyes frozen on his.

"Of course," he answered. "Forever."

"Forever," I confirmed. And our surroundings faded away as we slipped from the present and into the past. Forever was a long time. But I planned to spend every moment of it with Brennan. I opened my eyes.

Starting right now.

*THE END*

To read more of Em and Brennan, read book two of the Moonstone Saga, *Soul Bound.*

# Author's Notes

I always said I wouldn't write a vampire book. Not because I don't like to read them, because I do. I just think that there are so many good vamp stories already out there that I couldn't possibly add anything substantial to that genre. But in my defense, this isn't a vampire book. When I came across Empusa as I was doing research for the *Bloodstone Saga*, I knew that I not only wanted to use her in *The Bloodstone Saga*, but that I also wanted her to have her own series.

Why?

Because details surrounding her are so vague in Mythology…but just the sheer notion of who she is is exciting. Some legends list her as Hecate's consort and some list her as Hecate's daughter with Mormo. When I thought of her in that context, my writer's mind started spinning, building up a back-story and I went from there. Because actual details are so vague, it gives me a lot of creative leeway, which is music to a writer's ears. I could give her any kind of personality that I wished and that was so exciting to me.

And that's how Empusa's series was born.

In my version, as you just read, she is Hecate's daughter and she is beautiful, ethereal and has a backbone of steel. I can't wait to discover what other secrets she holds as I continue writing her. I hoped you enjoyed reading about her even half as much as I enjoy writing her.

*Soul Kissed*

# Acknowledgments

There are so many wonderful people in my life who support me in my writing life. My husband and my kids are so patient with me... when we have to have frozen pizza or takeout for dinner because I'm stuck in a scene or when I'm daydreaming about a character.

My mom is awesome- she reads everything that I write. Thanks, mom!

My fans are so amazingly awesome! I absolutely adore receiving your emails, tweets, Facebook messages, etc. You guys are the best fans in the world.

My Beta Readers ...Melissa, Shari, Ana, Meg, Em, Branwen. You guys totally rock my socks off! I don't know what I would do without your input.

My writerly friends... Michelle and Fisher. You guys are the best brainistorming/soundboards/talk-me-off-the-ledge friends ever. I don't know what I'd do without you.

And my bestie, Am.  Thanks for sticking with me ever since second grade.  (We won't mention exactly how long that has been!  Haha.)   I love you- always have, always will.